NAUGHTY HOUSEWIVES III

ERNEST MORRIS

GOOD2GO PUBLISHING

Naughty Housewives III
Written by Ernest Morris
Cover design: Davida Baldwin
Typesetter: Mychea
ISBN: 9781943686421

Copyright ©2016 Good2Go Publishing
Published 2016 by Good2Go Publishing
7311 W. Glass Lane • Laveen, AZ 85339
www.good2gopublishing.com
https://twitter.com/good2gobooks
G2G@good2gopublishing.com
www.facebook.com/good2gopublishing
www.instagram.com/good2gopublishing

ACKNOWLEDGMENTS

FIRST AND FOREMOST, I would like to once again give thanks to the man above for blessing me with the gift of writing. I couldn't have done this without you! The obstacles I faced trying to finish this novel are only the beginning compared to the ones ahead of me.

To the people at Good2Go Publishing working night and day to put my books out for the readers, thank you so much. If it wasn't for your hard work and dedication, none of this would be possible. It is because of you that my books are buzzing in the streets the way they are.

I would like to thank my readers for continuously supporting me through this journey that I've invested so much time in. You made me who I am today, and I truly appreciate that.

To all my family and friends at the Cheesecake Factory, thank you for having my back and always believing in me. Arnold, Dom, Evani, Pam, Kayla, Stacks, Marcus, A.J., Jalisa, Shelly, John, Will,

Mel, Rhonda, Ryan, Kyle, Torey, and everyone else holding it down out there, keep doing what you do. My new books called *The Factory*, and *Naughty Coeds* will be out in 2017, so look for them.

To my children, you're my inspiration to do what I do. I can't even explain how much I love you and always will.

To everyone else that I forgot to mention, thanks for the support!!

NAUGHTY HOUSEWIVES III

(Secrets Revealed)

PROLOGUE

AKIYLAH ARRIVED AT THE house in no time and parked in the driveway. There were so many questions going through her head that needed answering, but right now she just wanted to take a hot shower and put on some fresh clothes. One thing she was sure of was that regardless of what might happen between the two families, she wouldn't have to go back to being poor anymore. She walked in, kicked off her shoes, and proceeded upstairs to her and Sahmeer's bedroom. After undressing, she went into the bathroom and turned on the shower. She checked the temperature, making sure it was hot enough, then got in. The water was so soothing to her skin. She closed her eyes and enjoyed the sensation of it as it ran down her body.

Someone walked into the bathroom and just stood there watching her. He took off his clothes and stood by the sink, massaging his penis. Once it was fully hard, he walked over toward the shower and opened the door. Akiylah jumped, but when she saw who it was, a smile crept across her face.

"Me been waiting for you, baby," she said.

"Oh, is that right?" he replied, stepping inside and closing the door behind him.

Akiylah gave him a passionate kiss while rubbing on his erection. He squeezed her ass cheeks, then turned her around. Akiylah arched her back anticipating him entering her from behind. Not being able to hold back any longer, he entered her moist love box. She let out a soft moan, which almost caused him to ejaculate instantly.

"Me love you dick. It feels so good," she purposefully whined while moving her hips trying to match each stroke.

"Say my name if it's that good," he said, pumping in and out of her.

She was so caught up in the moment that she didn't hear a word he said to her. She was on the brink of having her first orgasm, when he stopped mid-stroke.

"I said say my name before I cum all over your ass," he repeated.

He began talking dirty to her, pulling her hair back, whispering in her hair. His aggressiveness was driving her crazy. She wanted to explode badly, and he was spoiling it for her right now. When she didn't respond, he repeated it again, this time biting her neck. Wanting him to continue so she could reach her climax, Akiylah said his name: "Mike, please just keep fucking me . . ."

ONE

MIKE CONTINUED TO FUCK Akiylah aggressively, until her juices poured out of her pussy each time he pulled back. Now Mike wanted to finish what he had started, so he stepped out of the shower, pulling her with him. They walked into the bedroom, and Akiylah hopped on the bed, spreading her legs wide open for him. Mike stood there momentarily, admiring how beautiful her pussy looked. The only other pussy that even stood a chance to hers was Sasha's, but just thinking about Sasha right now pissed him off.

He couldn't believe the news he got at the hospital. Was Sahmeer really his brother because his dad had an affair with Sasha? He put that thought in the back of his mind so he could focus on the naked woman lying on the bed in front of him.

"Come lick me clit," Akiylah said seductively, rubbing her middle finger over her tunnel.

That was his breaking point. He leaned over and placed her legs on his shoulders. Mike stuck one finger into her pussy, rotating it until he found her spot. When she started moaning uncontrollably, he picked up the speed, inserting his tongue as well.

"Yeessssss, baby, faster. That feels so good. Don't stop," she screamed out. Her pussy was on fire and needed something else to put out the flames.

Mike's tongue worked its way up to her lips, and he kissed her, letting her taste her own juices. Another moan escaped her mouth when she felt his hand make contact with her swollen nipples. She opened her eyes so she could watch him perform. Each time he kissed her nipples, it was slow and sensual as if he was a pro. She wondered why she didn't pick him first. It was obvious that he was more experienced at pleasing a woman orally than Sahmeer was.

Her right hand found his erection, and she gently stroked it, rubbing the tip with care. She felt his dick start pulsating in her hand, and she wanted it inside her soaked pussy.

"Me want to feel you back inside me," she said, pulling him up to her so his dick was level with her opening.

Mike didn't waste any more time teasing her. He started off slowly when he entered her, then sped up like he was in a rush. Akiylah felt every inch of his girth as he worked overtime on her. The bed was bouncing up and down from the pounding he was putting on her.

"Right there, baby. That's my spot," Akiylah cried out in pleasure. Her pussy was so wet that it made squishy noises each time Mike's dick went in and out.

"I'm about to cum, baby," Mike moaned.

"Cum inside me, please. I want to have your baby," she replied, holding onto his waist so he wouldn't pull out.

Mike thought about it for a second before realizing that wouldn't be a good idea. He pulled out just in time to explode all over her stomach. She smeared it all over her body as she watched him stroke his manhood to get all his sperm out. When he was done, he sat on the edge of the bed checking his phone. Akiylah wrapped her arms around him, kissing his neck.

"When will me see you again?" she pouted.

"Soon but you have to hurry up and get back to the hospital to be by Sahmeer's side. He needs you there right now. We can't let no one find out our secret either. When the time is right, I promise you that we'll be together," he said, pulling her around so she was now straddling him. He squeezed her ass cheeks together while his mouth found its way to her nipples.

"As much as me don't want you to stop, me have to take another shower and get back to me husband," Akiylah said softly, holding the back of his head.

Mike released his grip and lifted Akiylah up off of him. She headed toward the shower, and he slipped his clothes back on. There was some place he had to be, and it wasn't back at that hospital. Between Sasha and Kevin, he had ten calls. He knew what his dad wanted, but why was Sasha calling so much? It was her idea to end their affair in the first place. He rushed out the door hoping that no one was pulling up to the house. Instead of returning any of their calls, he decided to go home and take a nap. He would deal with the maternity thing later.

* * *

Kevin woke up first, looking around the room. He had fallen asleep from the exhaustion of giving up so much blood. Sasha was sitting next to Sahmeer's bed, holding his hand when she noticed Kevin's eyes open. She kissed Sahmeer's hand and then walked over to Kevin.

"How are you feeling?" she asked.

"Tired! How is he doing?" Kevin replied.

"The doctor said the medicine will have him out for a few hours. Once it wears off, we'll know for sure if he's okay."

"That's good. Can you give me a glass of water? My mouth is dry as hell," Kevin said, sitting up. Sasha walked into the bathroom to get him a glass of water. When she came back out, Kevin was flipping through the TV channels. She gave him the water, then sat down in the chair next to the bed.

"Listen, I'm sorry for everything that has happened. I shouldn't have kept this from you this long," Sasha said.

"Sasha I'm not the one you should be apologizing to. What happened between us was a long time ago, and we were both kids. We hurt Marcus, Sahmeer, and Mike, though. They are the ones who deserve an apology from both of us."

"Yeah, you're right, but I didn't expect it to come out like this. I should have said something a long time ago. Maybe it wouldn't have been so bad," she said as tears fell down her face. She got up and walked over to the window, staring out.

"Stop being so hard on yourself. Everything will work itself out," he said, standing up and walking toward her. She continued looking out the window.

He put his hands around her and gave her a hug. Sasha could feel his dick pressing against her ass. She had on sweatpants because she wanted to be comfortable in the hospital so she felt his thickness poking at her. It was actually starting to feel good to her. When his body moved a little, her kitty got wet.

Sasha moved away from him, trying not to take it there with him. She knew if she stayed in his arms any longer, she would end up bent over the bathroom toilet getting her back knocked out. Kevin turned around and watched her walk back over to where Sahmeer was.

"Did you ever think about what we could have been if we ended up together?" he asked, following behind her.

"I don't think about stuff like that Kevin. We have our own families to take care of now, so let's just focus on that. Besides, we have to all sit down and talk about this when Sahmeer is feeling better. It's going to be hard on all of us, and we have to put our differences to the side and do what's best for the kids."

"Sasha, the kids are grown now. I'm sure they can handle this just fine. It's Marcus I'm worried about. I don't know how he's going to take the fact that his best friend is also his son's father. You seen the look on his face when the doctor told him. I thought he was going to kill me," Kevin replied.

"I wish Michelle was still here so I could explain everything to her. It's just not right that she's gone. I miss her so much," she said.

"I know. I miss her too. I feel better now, so I'm ready to get the hell out of this place. Can you grab the doctor and ask him for my discharge papers? I'm going to call Mike to come pick me up while you do that," Kevin replied, searching for his cell phone.

Sasha left the room to look for the doctor to come make sure Kevin was healthy enough to leave. Kevin called his son, then got dressed. While he was tying up his shoes, he heard a soft moan coming from Sahmeer's direction. He looked up and saw his eyes open, looking around. Kevin smiled and walked over to him, touching him on the arm.

"Where is my mom and dad?" Sahmeer asked in a groggy voice.

"Your mom stepped out for a moment to get the doctor, and your dad should be back soon also," Kevin stated, not wanting to tell him the news just yet. Even though he was his biological father, he felt like it wasn't his place to deliver that kind of news.

"What about my wife?"

"She went home to change clothes."

Sasha walked back into the room, followed by the doctor. When she saw Sahmeer sitting up, tears began falling from her eyes. She ran to her son and hugged him so tightly that he thought he was going to suffocate. He also held his mother tightly.

"I'm so glad you are okay. You have no idea what we have been going through in these last couple of days," Sasha told him.

"I thought I was going to die when that shark gripped my leg. It was so fucking big, and there was more than one," Sahmeer replied. "When will I be able to go home, Mom?"

"Soon, and watch your mouth, I'm still your mother. I'm waiting for the doctor to say it's okay for you to leave, so just be patient, okay? They just want to keep you under observation for awhile."

Sasha stayed with Sahmeer until Marcus came back. Then she left to let them talk. She had pulled Marcus to the side and asked him not to say anything until Sahmeer was better, and Marcus agreed. No matter what, he was still Sahmeer's father, and nothing was going to change that.

TWO

MORGAN HAD TAKEN OVER as the new Pennsylvania governor because of the sudden illness that had taken over the current governor. There were a lot of changes he wanted to make in the laws, especially the ones in the prison system, but he was going to wait until after the presidential election. Since he was a Democrat, he was rooting for Hillary Clinton to win. He liked what Trump was saying, but it felt like he was doing it for publicity. Either way anyone voted, there would be a controversy, but Clinton was the best fit for our country.

Morgan was sitting at his desk going over his agenda for the day when his new secretary walked in. She was very attractive and had a beautiful body. Her name was Carmelita. She was Cambodian and black, stood five foot two with long hair that came to her waist, and had a tongue ring that he wanted her to use on his shaft. She stared at him with those emerald-green eyes, causing his dick to come to life.

"Good morning, sir. I am your new secretary. If you need anything at all, just give me a buzz. I'll be right outside at my desk," she said before turning to leave.

Morgan looked at the way her skirt was wrapped around her firm ass, and smiled. He thought about the way she said it, and it sounded as if she was flirting with him. Just to be sure, he decided to try his hand. "Hey, when did you start?"

"Yesterday! I was supposed to be assigned to the other governor, but his condition . . ." she drifted off, thinking about what happened. "Now I'm assigned to you, and to be honest, I'd rather work for you."

"Why is that?" he said, never taking his eyes off her cleavage.

"Who wouldn't want to work for a handsome man like yourself," she replied, licking her cherry-covered lips.

Morgan couldn't resist this woman standing in his office right now. He wanted to get up under that skirt she had on. He stood up and walked around the desk to get a better view.

"So you think I'm handsome, huh?" he said, sitting on the edge. He knew getting involved with another secretary wasn't a good idea, but once again his dick was speaking for him.

"I do, sir," she said, walking over to him and straightening his tie.

She was standing so close to him that he thought he felt the heat coming from her body. She was feeling frisky too; it was her plan the whole time. She leaned in and whispered into his ear. "Would you like me to show you how handsome you are?" She now stood between his legs and could feel his erection coming from his pants.

He gripped her by the waist and slid his hand down to her ass, squeezing its firmness. Carmelita let out a soft moan and wrapped her arms around his neck. Morgan stood up and walked around back to his seat, pulling Carmelita with him. She sat on his lap and stuck her tongue in his mouth. The whole time he kissed her, his hands were groping every part of her body.

She slid out of his lap and onto her knees in front of him. Unzipping his pants, she reached inside and removed his penis. Carmelita puckered her lips, then seductively blew on the tip of it, making it grow even larger than it was. Morgan pulled her up, starting to feel slightly guilty about what they were doing. She leaned over and licked inside his ear with her tongue, sending goose bumps all over his body.

"Miss, you tripping right now," he whispered. "Damn, that shit feels good."

"I feel it too, baby," she cooed, inconspicuously rubbing his package. Any guilt he was feeling before had instantly rescinded from his mind. "You like this, don't you?"

"Definitely," he replied, closing his eyes.

"Well your gonna love this," she stated, wrapping her hand around his length, then inserting it into her warm mouth in one swift motion.

That was some freaky shit, and he loved every moment of it. The way she worked her mouth had him thinking it was her pussy. He couldn't hold his semen in any longer.

"I'm about to cum," he moaned.

Just as he was releasing his semen into Carmelita's mouth, the door to his office opened and, in came Det. Davis. He had a smug smile on his face. Morgan pushed his secretary's head down so the detective couldn't see her.

"What are you doing all the way down here, and why didn't you call first?" Morgan asked, looking up at the detective.

"I thought I would drop in and say hello. You don't look too good, Governor, are you okay?" he replied.

"Yes, I'm just finishing up so I can go to lunch."

"You sure it's not the accommodation you just received?"

Morgan looked up at the detective with a shocked look on his face.

"Sir, I'm a detective. This is what I do."

Morgan was caught with his pants down once again and just shook his head. Without saying a word, he pulled his chair back so his secretary could get up from under the desk. She fixed her clothes as she walked out of the office.

Det. Davis stared at the beautiful woman as she walked out. "That's a fine piece of meat you have there. I see someone just can't keep it in their pants. You need to get you an old fat secretary. Then you won't have to worry about sticking your dick where it don't belong," Det. Davis smirked.

"You don't worry about what's going on in my office. Just tell me why you're here."

"I told you that I would be cashing in on a favor. Well it's time to pay up, boss," the detective said.

"Detective Davis, what is it that you want?"

"Call me Pete, and how about we go to lunch together and I'll explain everything to you, sir." He started walking toward the door.

Morgan fixed his clothes and grabbed his briefcase. As they walked out the door, he whispered something to Carmelita, then headed out with the detective. She smiled and continued her work.

* * *

"How's everything going with you?" Raphael said to Carla.

"It's been stressful, but I think I'll be okay after the divorce is final," she replied.

Carla and Raphael had kept in contact since their last session, but Carla never told him about testing positive for the HIV virus. That was something she just didn't have enough courage to do. Before things got too serious between them, she would let him know. They were sitting in T.G.I. Friday's on City Line Avenue, having dinner.

"If there's anyone that deserves happiness, it's you. He never deserved you from the start, Carla," Raphael said, grabbing her by the hand. He gently ran his finger up and down her palm, sending shockwaves throughout her body, especially the spot between her legs. She had to let go before she let go of something else.

"You always know what to say to make me smile," Carla replied.

"I say it because it's true. Carla, ever since that day you came to the center and asked me to teach you how to play the piano, I have fantasized about you. I've wanted you in the worst way. I didn't care who your husband was then, and I don't care now.

If the people knew what he done to you, he wouldn't even be the governor, or anything else, for that matter."

"Listen, Raphael, I don't want to discuss my ex. Let's change the subject, please," she said, getting irritated.

He understood what she was saying and quickly switched the conversation. They talked and enjoyed their meal for the next hour, before departing. Raphael followed her back to her house to make sure she got there safely. She invited him in for a drink, and he accepted. They talked some more, and then Raphael got up to leave.

"I had fun with you tonight, Carla. I can't wait to see you again." He gave her a hug, and before she knew it, they were kissing.

It wasn't a little peck either. It was hot and steamy with a lot of tongue. His hand slipped down from her waist to her ass, and he caressed it. Carla was in so much heat and needed the fire between her legs put out immediately.

"Do you want to go upstairs?" she asked, out of breath. She figured they could use a condom and everything would be alright.

This was the opportunity that Raphael had been waiting for. He definitely wasn't going to blow this chance. He followed her up to the bedroom, staring at her ass the whole way and taking in her scent. No words were said as they entered the room and Carla closed the door behind her. But she couldn't go through with it until she told him her secret.

"Raphael, there's something I need to tell you before we go that route." When he didn't say anything, she continued. "I'm just going to come straight out with it: my husband gave me the HIV virus," she said, taking a deep breath. She expected him to go rushing out the door, but he stayed there.

"Carla, for any other man, that might be a problem. I'm not like any other man, though. I've been in love with you for so long that I don't care what's wrong with you. We can work this out together, baby, 'cause I want you here and now."

Carla looked at him in total shock as tears formed in her eyes. Raphael walked up to her and wrapped his arms around her. He kissed her on the forehead, then wiped the tears away. She backed away from him smiling. She was going to give him what they both needed tonight. He sat down on the bed and watched as she started removing her clothes one piece at a time. Carla walked over toward where he was sitting, never taking her eyes off of his, and wrapped her body around his. He could smell her essence when her legs opened. He smiled when she showed him the condom.

Raphael took the liberty of spreading her lower lips and dipping his finger into her hole, giving it a slow stir before bringing it to his lips, sucking it clean. He closed his eyes as her sweetness coated his tongue, and he felt like he had died and gone to heaven.

Lying back on the bed, he rolled her off of him then stood up to take off his clothes. His penis sprang free from his boxers immediately, ready to dive in her hot spot. He rolled back to get between her thighs. Pre-cum stained the comforter as he made contact with the bed. The pulse that flowed through his midsection had him about to lose his damn mind, but he first needed to taste her.

He had been waiting, fantasizing, and dreaming about this moment for way too long to let it slip away now. Opening her legs even wider, she spread her lips for him, causing her clit to pop out. He slurped it up greedily, plunging into her tight hole with his tongue. Raphael dug his fingers into her juicy ass cheeks, loving the firmness of them. Finally he was getting the chance to make love to Carla, and now he was going to devour her body.

Their bodies were on fire as she pushed him out of the way and placed her body over his in the sixty-nine position. It felt like he'd submerged his dick in lava when her mouth covered it, and it made him almost coat her tonsils with his semen on contact. She placed her neatly trimmed pussy on his mouth, and he ate it like a starving maniac.

"Mmmm," he moaned out in between licks, "I'm gonna bust, baby. You have to stop doing that for a minute."

She ignored him as her mouth and tongue worked the underside of his manhood down to that little space beneath his balls. Her hands were massaging his sac in the process. He didn't think he would be able to hold on any longer. He lifted her naked body up and positioned her over him in a backward riding position. She took the cue, removing the condom from its wrapper and sliding it down his shaft. She then slid her body down onto it, milking him with her tight walls.

It was agonizingly delicious as she worked him. He held tightly to her hips, meeting her every thrust. Leaning up a little, he wrapped his arm around her body to find her clit. Using the tip of his finger, he stroked her slowly at first, building up a rhythm as it stiffened under his touch, indicating that she was about to blow. They moaned in unison as his cream began to rise to the top as well. Her walls felt so good around his dick. He dug deep trying to knock the bottom out of her pussy. It was so juicy and tight, and her warm body felt extremely good pressed up against him.

She dug her nails into his thighs as his fingertips played across her clit. He could feel it pulsate as her walls clinched and unclinched around him. They both went into convulsions as she bore down on him and they both shot off at the same time. They lay there trying to get themselves together for a few minutes.

"Wow, that was probably the best sex I ever had," Raphael stated, playing with her hair. She was lying on his chest.

"Probably the best?" she questioned, looking up at him.

"I'm just playing with you," he replied, kissing her on the forehead.

"Whatever you say." She playfully punched him in the arm. "I like what we have right now. Just don't hurt me like he did."

"I won't, and that's a promise," he said. "Now let me get some more of this good stuff." He grabbed another condom out of the box, and they made love for the rest of the night. Carla was in heaven, but she would soon find out that every good thing comes to an end.

THREE

SYMIRA HAD JUST ARRIVED to her gynecologist appointment and was sitting in the room waiting for her doctor, when her phone rang. It was her sister sending her a text message. Symira texted her back, then turned the ringer off because the doctor walked in.

"Good afternoon, Symira. I hope I didn't keep you waiting too long," he said, closing the door.

"No, I just got here," she replied, leaning back on the table so he could begin his examination. He washed his hands, then put on some gloves while sitting at the edge of the table next to the wall. She placed her feet up on the stirrups and opened her legs as wide as she could. The doctor squirted some jelly on his gloved fingers so he could examine her vagina. She flinched a little when he stuck his finger inside. He moved it around for a minute before pulling out.

"It looks like everything is fine. You are about eighteen weeks pregnant. I want you to continue taking your prenatal vitamins and working out, okay?"

Symira nodded her head, hoping that he would stick his finger back inside her pussy because it was feeling so good before he stopped. He didn't though. He stood up, removing his gloves, then wrote something down in her file. She was pregnant but didn't know if the father was Morgan or her husband. What she did know was that it didn't matter because she was going to say that it was Morgan's, in the hopes that he would take her back.

"Check with the nurse at the desk for your next appointment after you get dressed. Will there be anything else?"

She wanted to say, "Yes can you make me cum before you go," but didn't. "No, I'll see you at my next appointment."

"Okay, if you need anything, you have my cell phone number. Just call and I'll come to you," he said, leaving the room so she could put her clothes on. Her pussy was throbbing for some attention, and there was no one to give it to her right now. One of her toys would have to do.

"I sure will," she said to herself as she slipped into her tights.

After she left the doctor's office, she stopped at the Cheesecake Factory to get something to eat. She decided to do some shopping afterward since she was at Christiana Mall in Newark, Delaware. The restaurant was a little crowded, but Symira's sister worked there, so due to the cancellation of a reservation, she was able to get a corner table. One of the waitresses came over to take her order.

"Hi, my name is Kayla, and I will be your server today. What would you like to drink?" she asked, handing Symira a menu.

Symira scanned the menu quickly, then placed her order. Kayla walked away to get her food while Symira looked around in search for her sister. Symira noticed one of the servers staring at her. She looked familiar, and it only took Symira a second to realize who it was. She smiled as the server walked toward her.

"Symira, I knew that was you. How have you been?" Nancy asked.

Nancy and Symira went to the same school together. They even had their first girl-on-girl action together when they were roommates in college. Their friendship kind of faded when Nancy moved out of Delaware. Symira noticed how big her ass got and wanted to touch it.

"I've been okay. What are you doing working here?"

"I went back to school, so this is one of the ways I make some extra money," Nancy replied, sitting down across from her.

"I thought you would be out in California somewhere making movies with some famous people. What happened to your acting career?" Symira asked.

"It kind of flopped when I stayed with someone I thought I was in love with. He ended up running off with some executive director that got some job in Florida," Nancy said with distaste in her mouth.

Symira knew who she was referring to because he made a pass at her that same night they all were at a dormitory party. She quickly shut him down because she was dating Morgan at the time and she was loyal.

"Stand up and turn around. I want to see how big your ass got," Symira said playfully, trying to change the subject. "Is it real?"

"This is all real right here," Nancy told her, standing up, smiling at her. "This is what a little back shots will get you. I have to get back to work, but what are you doing in an hour?"

"Nothing. Why? What's up?"

"There's this bar on Main Street called Deer Park. Do you want to go hang out with me and my friend? She works at that apartment complex on Elkton Road called Studio Green. We can catch up and have some fun."

"Sure, just give me a call when you're ready. I'm going to go pick up something to wear," she re-plied, giving Nancy her number.

Symira left out as Nancy went to serve her tables. She stopped at the mall and found something to wear, then headed over to her friend's house to get dressed. She was excited to be going out to have some fun even though she couldn't drink. Symira checked her phone and saw a text from her doctor. It said that he needed to do another sonogram as soon as possible. She wondered why, but decided to call him tomorrow morning. Tonight she was going to have fun.

* * *

Deer Park was packed when they walked in. They walked over to the bar and ordered drinks, then headed to the second floor to find Nancy's friend. Symira checked her friend out the whole way up the steps. She was mesmerized by how big her ass was in that next-to-nothing dress she had on. The music was jumping as people partied away on the dance floor. Nancy's friend was grinding on some guy in the middle of the floor. They should have been having sex the way they were dancing. As Symira and Nancy approached Nancy's friend, Symira felt someone step behind her, grabbing her waist. He was trying to dance with her, and his friend pulled Nancy toward him. At first Symira didn't want to dance, but the way the guy's manhood felt on her ass, she changed her mind.

She began doing a sensual dance, letting the guy know she wasn't a slouch. The whole time they danced, her eyes never left Nancy, who was staring at her. Symira felt her pussy moistening once again. Nancy grabbed her hand, and they both started moving their hips as the men kept dancing with them.

After a couple of songs played, they walked over and stood by the wall. Nancy's friend walked over to introduce herself to Symira.

"Hey, girl, " she said, giving Nancy a hug. She then turned to Symira. "Hi, I'm Annabel. It's nice to finally meet you. You are really beautiful."

"Thank you," Symira replied, blushing.

"Well, I know you two didn't just come here to stand on the wall. Let's have some fun," Nancy stated, grabbing them both by the hand and pulling them out to the dance floor.

All three women danced to the music like they were the only people there. Different men tried to approach them, but they just brushed them off.

Symira was really enjoying herself with the two gorgeous women. Nancy went to use the bathroom, so Symira and Annabel sat down in one of the booths, still bopping to the sounds of Drake's "Energy."

"You are rocking the shit out of that red leather skirt. It makes you look sexy as hell," Annabel said, staring at Symira.

That comment made Symira blush and feel all gooey inside. Annabel slid closer to her, and Symira squeezed her legs together, trying to stop the juices that were trying to escape her love box. Since she started taking those prenatal vitamins, her hormones were at an all-time high. Annabel was a very beautiful white girl with long black hair. She was five foot seven, 150 pounds, with nice perky breasts and a nice ass. Symira also admired Annabel's body because there weren't too many white girls with natural bodies like hers. Usually it took a plastic surgeon to create a masterpiece like that.

"Thank you again for the compliment. You better not drink anymore tonight," Symira replied, noticing how buzzed Annabel was.

Annabel placed a hand on Symira's leg, sending a chill throughout her body. Annabel began rubbing it, moving closer up her thigh toward her kitty cat. Symira closed her eyes, enjoying Annabel's touch.

"Damn, your legs are smooth. I wonder if something else is also," Annibel whispered in Symira's ear, sticking her tongue inside and licking her earlobe.

When Annabel's hand reached her spot, Annabel realized Symira didn't have any panties on. She stuck one, then two fingers inside, fingering her pussy. Symira opened her eyes and gave her a wicked smile.

"I hate wearing any," she said, opening her legs a little to give Annabel's fingers more access. Annabel pulled her fingers out and stuck them in her mouth, tasting the sweet liquid. She kept rolling her fingers around her tongue making sure she sucked it all off. When she placed them back inside Symira's pussy, Symira started rotating her hips to the rhythm of each stroke.

"I see I'm missing all the fun," Nancy smirked as she returned to the table. Both women looked up at their friend. She sat down across from them, taking a sip of her drink. "How about we all just get out of here and go back to my place?"

"How far do you live from here?" Symira asked, fixing her skirt as she stood up.

"We can go to my place. It's closer," Annabel replied. Besides working at Studio Green, she also had an apartment there.

They all left the bar in a hurry so they could go back to Annabel's crib to have some girl fun. All of them had been with other women before, so they knew what was about to go down. Symira didn't know that Annabel and Nancy had been messing around for six months now and had set this up earlier when she came to eat at her job. They followed behind Annabel to her apartment. When they all went inside, Annabel put on some music as they all got comfortable. She had this giant king-size bed that looked like it was made to roll around on. Nancy started doing a striptease dance for them.

"Do you like the way she's dancing?" Annabel asked Symira as she rubbed her titties.

Annabel stood up and started undressing right in front of her. Nancy sat down in a chair across from them to watch the show. Annabel's body was flawless from head to toe. She had a Brazilian bikini waxed pussy, and Symira's mouth watered with anticipation to suck on her pretty clit. Annabel lay on the bed, spread eagle, and started playing with herself.

"Hey, why don't you come over here and put your pussy right on my face?" she asked Symira. The way she said it made Symira have an orgasm.

Symira stood over her face, raising her skirt and lowering her pussy onto Annabel's face. She started rubbing it back and forth over her mouth, enjoying the friction that it was creating.

"Oh, yes, suck my pussy. That feels so good," Symira moaned.

She started pinching her nipples, pushing them close together, then sucking on them one at a time. Nancy stuck her hand inside her panties and began playing with her pussy as she watched the two women explore each other's bodies. She took all her clothes off, placing one leg over the arm of the chair for easier access, then listened to the moaning sounds they were making as she reached her own climax.

"Why don't you come join us in bed?" Symira requested, turning her body around so they were in the sixty-nine position.

Nancy walked over to the bed seductively, rubbing her titties. Her nipples were at least one inch long and were pierced. Symira thought she could see the radiant heat coming from Nancy's body when she sat down next to them. Symira was licking and fingering Annabel while Nancy stuck two fingers into Symira's ass. It caused her to have orgasm after orgasm, and her body shook uncontrollably.

Symira all of a sudden felt Nancy's warm tongue enter her asshole. It drove her so crazy that she sped up the pace on Annabel. Her pussy tasted like cherries, and it was so wet. They took turns with each other all night, trying every position until they couldn't take it anymore. Nancy fucked Symira, Symira fucked Annabel, and Annabel fucked Nancy.

"I have to get home before my man gets mad," Nancy said as she looked at the clock. It was five o'clock in the morning.

All three women were soaking wet from sweating. Symira's hormones were still going crazy, but she knew she also had to get home. She had a meeting with her lawyer that morning to discuss the settlement between her and her husband.

"Can I take a quick shower?" Symira asked.

"I think we all should take a quick shower," replied Nancy as she headed for the bathroom.

"Y'all go ahead. I have to make a few calls. There are fresh towels and washcloths in the drawer. If you need anything else, let me know," Annabel told them.

As soon as they left the room, Annabel made a few calls. She kept her eyes on the bathroom door the whole time, making sure no one came out in the middle of her conversation. After getting dressed, Symira headed back to Philly and Nancy went home to get some rest before work. Annabel looked over toward the alarm clock sitting on the dresser and smiled, thinking about what she planned on doing sooner or later.

FOUR

KEVIN WAS SITTING IN the back of his house drinking a beer, looking over toward Sasha's house. He was still thinking about the chain of events that changed both families' lives. Sahmeer was his son all this time, and she had held that from him. In his mind, he wanted to tell Sahmeer, but he had promised Sasha he would wait until the time was right. The sound of his doorbell interrupted his thoughts. Kevin looked at the monitor on his phone to see who was there. It was Marcus, so he buzzed him in.

"I'm out back, Marcus," he yelled out to his neighbor, teammate, and most importantly, friend. Marcus walked out, grabbed a beer from the refrigerator sitting next to Kevin, and sat down. No words were spoken for what seemed like an eternity. Then Marcus broke the silence.

"I wanted to let you know that this will not alter our friendship in any way. We will get through this, bro."

"I know, but I still feel like I owe you an explanation for the mistake I made when we were younger," Kevin stated, putting the bottle down.

"That's just it, Kevin: we were all teenagers having fun. We had no clue we would be with them today," Marcus replied.

He was thinking about how Michelle must be turning in her grave right now knowing the deception that her husband and best friend had kept a secret all these years. The two of them talked for a few minutes before heading to practice. This was their last season playing in the NBA, and they wanted to go out on top this year.

Marcus had found out that Lebron and the Cavs had been inquiring about him because they needed a shooter, but they couldn't reach an agreement yet. New York had been in search for a defensive player to help Noah and Porzingis in the paint, and the Sixers' coaching staff wasn't trying to give him up that easy.

"What do you think about us being traded to different teams?" Kevin asked as they shot the ball around.

"If it happens then I guess we will have to deal with it. It would mean that both of us would still be on the East Coast and would play each other," Marcus said.

"Then I can show you that I am the better player between us," Kevin joked as the coach blew his whistle, indicating that it was time to watch films of their opponents for their upcoming game tomorrow.

They usually ran a scrimmage game before the meeting, but the coach decided not to do that today. Everyone sat in the film room as the assistant coach went over different strategies.

"Marcus and Kevin, I would like to speak with you in my office," the coach requested.

They already knew what it was about, so they both got up and followed him. They were only in there for ten minutes before coming out. Both had disappointed looks on their faces, but they also looked relieved. They would both be staying in Philadelphia right now until someone gave them a good deal. Marcus wanted to retire with this organization because of all the years he had put in.

On the other hand, Kevin was ready to go. He wanted a championship, and if he stayed here, it wasn't going to happen. Even with their new additions, they didn't stand a chance against a team like Cleveland, New York, Boston, or any other team, for that matter. They finished practice for the day, and Kevin left to meet up with a friend. Marcus decided to head to the hospital because his son was being released today and he wanted to be there to pick him up.

* * *

Sasha and Akiylah were sitting in the room waiting for Sahmeer to get dressed. He was finally being released from the hospital, and everyone was excited. Marcus walked in pushing the wheelchair for his son. Even though Sahmeer protested, it was the hospital's policy that a patient that's being discharged must be escorted out in a wheelchair. Sahmeer didn't mind as long as he was getting out of that place.

"Can we stop and get something to eat? After eating hospital food all this time, I want some real food," Sahmeer said, sitting in the backseat of his dad's car.

"Whatever you want, baby," Sasha replied.

Akiylah and Marcus got in, and they drove to Applebee's to eat. It wasn't as crowded, because it was only a little after twelve, but people were starting to come in. They sat down at the table and waited for the waitress to take their order. Sasha kept staring at Marcus like she could guess what he was thinking. The truth was, she could. She knew that he was looking at all of Sahmeer's features, wondering if he wasn't his, how come he still looked just like him.

"How are you feeling, buddy?" Marcus asked his son.

"I'll be feeling a whole lot better when that steak comes."

Everyone started laughing at his answer. It felt good that all the tension between them had calmed down some. Even Akyilah and Marcus had kind of come to an understanding. Sahmeer couldn't be mad at his dad anymore after seeing that his wife was willing to forgive him. He would forgive, but he wouldn't forget.

"Here it comes," Sasha replied, watching the waitress place their food on the table.

Everyone ate and talked like a real family. Sasha's phone went off indicating that she had a text message. She read it then looked around, searching for someone. As soon as they locked eyes, she nodded her head and held up her hand to say "one minute."

"Excuse me, I have to make a call real quick," Sasha said, standing up.

"Is everything alright, Mom?" Sahmeer questioned.

"Yes, baby, it's my friend having a small crisis right now, and she needs my advice. I'm going to use the ladies' room. I'll be right back."

Sasha headed toward the restroom area that was located in the back, away from her family. She stood there waiting by the wall, when the door to the diaper changing room opened. Sasha stepped inside closing the door behind her, then taking a deep breath.

"Sorry if I'm disturbing your family time. I was sitting over there with my friend and noticed y'all were here."

"What's so important that you couldn't just come over there and join us? I've been trying to talk to you about this situation, but you left before I had a chance."

"Is it really true about you and my dad?" Mike asked, looking like he wanted to cry.

Sasha held her head down in shame momentarily, then looked up at him. She could see the hurt look on his face, but the past was the past.

"We were all young and reckless back then. Now we must all get over this and move forward with our lives."

"Have you told him yet?" he said, leaning on the sink.

"No, we're waiting for the right time to talk to him. I would appreciate if you wouldn't say anything either."

"I'm not going to say nothing. I can't believe that he's my real brother. So why were you looking for me and blowing my phone up?" he asked, moving closer to Sasha.

She could feel the tension between the two of them and wanted to run out of there, but her legs wouldn't move. He grabbed her waist and kissed her passionately. She melted like butter into his arms. His tongue gently prodded hers hard and deep. He slowly unbuttoned her blouse and slid it off her shoulders, revealing her swelling nipples. Mike pinched one between his fingers then cupped them together with both hands, slowly licking them up and down. He teased each hardened nipple with flicks of his tongue. Still holding her breasts together, he buried his face between her flesh.

"I have to get back before they come looking for me," she moaned softly.

"Just a few minutes longer," he replied, sliding off his jeans.

He lifted up her skirt, sliding her damp panties to the side. He kissed her again, sliding his finger into her wet pussy. His finger caressed her vagina as he rubbed her slit. When he inserted another finger into her cunt and rested his thumb on her clit, Sasha squealed out in joy.

Sasha felt the climax building up within her, and her breathing grew faster and heavy. His fingers thrashed in and out of her pussy as she was overtaken by an orgasm that left her shaking. Mike smiled at her as she came, and before she had fully recovered, he lifted her up on the diaper changing table and kissed her clit, sending her into another heart-racing orgasm. He stroked her pussy and kissed her thighs as she came back down to earth. She came so hard that she could hardly move.

"Now you can go back to your family," Mike said, putting his pants back on. He didn't even try to fuck her.

Sasha was horny as hell right now and wanted some dick. She reached out to him, but he moved away and walked out the door, leaving her there with a wet pussy. Mike smiled as he headed toward his table. He wasn't planning on doing that, but he couldn't pass up the chance to get back at her for leaving him like she did. He knew she would come running back for more, and he would definitely be waiting. He was playing a dangerous game with her and Akiylah, but didn't care.

* * *

Det. Davis and Morgan had come to an agreement to make Det. Davis the new deputy commissioner, but it wasn't as easy as Morgan thought it would be. Morgan had to persuade the mayor to be on board, or else it wouldn't happen. Being the governor, he could just order him to do it, but he'd rather take a subtle approach first.

"So this is the whole breakdown for the changes I want to make. Of course I would run it by our PC (police commissioner) first. These are the people I would like to promote and give new assignments to," the detective said, passing a folder to the mayor and Morgan.

"I see you have it all figured out. We will look everything over and get back to you in a week or two," the mayor replied, looking through the file the detective gave them. "I have to run this idea by my committee first, but I think it will work."

"Thank you, Mayor, and I will see you this weekend for golf?" Morgan stated, walking the mayor to the door.

"You sure will, Governor. See you later, Detective, or should I say Deputy Commissioner?" the mayor said, closing the door.

Morgan walked over and sat down at his desk. He was responsible for changing Det. Davis's personnel files. All the complaints had been erased, and he added a few decorative accommodations to it. He made the detective seem like a great cop, instead of the lowdown scum he was. Morgan would have never jeopardized himself if the detective hadn't had dirt on him. Det. Davis was holding the chips for now, and he had to accept that.

"Well I guess that concludes our meeting for today. Are you heading back to Philly, or you staying out here for another day?" Morgan asked, hoping Det. Davis would leave ASAP.

"I was going to stay until tomorrow since I took three days of vacation time. I'll be heading back in the morning. If you need to reach me, I'll be at the

Marriott International," Det. Davis replied, shaking Morgan's hand.

When he walked out the door heading toward the elevator, Morgan's secretary walked by switching. He stared at her ass, but this time discretely touching it. Carmelita gave him a seductive look that instantly caused him an erection.

"Watch your hands before you bite off more than you can chew," she said, spinning around to face him.

"I would sure like to see that. Here is my room number at the Marriott International. Come have dinner with me tonight. I'm leaving in the morning and don't known when I'll be back," he said, writing down his info on a piece of paper. She took it and stuck it in her jacket pocket.

"I'm spending time with my friends, but maybe afterward I'll stop by," she told him as he stepped into the elevator.

"Bring them with you if you like. We can all have some fun. There is a big-ass pool on the roof that we can swim in. Think about it," he said as the door closed behind him.

FIVE

DET. DAVIS, BETTER KNOWN as Pete, sat near the pool waiting for Carmelita and her two friends to change their clothes and join him. He met them at the bar earlier, and they all had drinks and talked for a while. During that time, Pete found out that Carmelita used to strip to pay for college. She had a degree in public relations and was hoping to soon become the governor's personal assistant. What she didn't tell him was that she would do anything to get what she wanted, even if meant fucking very powerful men. Although he didn't have status yet, she knew that he was important because of the meeting he had with her boss earlier.

When they walked out to the pool, Pete was glad he had a towel over his lap. It hid the erection threatening to break through it. All three of them were wearing the skimpiest bikinis you could imagine. They walked over and sat next to him by the pool.

"What would you like to drink?" he asked the ladies.

"It doesn't matter, just make it a double," Sokda, one of Carmelita's friends, replied.

Sokda Hun was a Cambodian goddess. She was five foot five, had long black hair, and was petite, with a face that looked like Pocahontas's. She had a ring in both her nose and tongue. Her eyes were slanted, and she always switched up her hair color. Pete wanted a piece of her badly.

Their other friend was just as pretty. Her name was Tina Wu. At five foot four, with perky lips, a milk-chocolate complexion, short-length hair, and a bubble ass, she should have been a model. She was Sokda's cousin, and you could see the resemblance.

They all had a few drinks and were really tipsy. Suddenly Pete felt hands go over his eyes and a leg wrap around his body. A pair of soft lips gently kissed his while another pair of arms eased under the shirt he had on. He sat there flabbergasted, with a hard-on that was now working its way through the leg of his shorts. He was ready for all three of the beauties to get naked.

"I see that I'm not the only one ready to have some fun," Pete said, cupping Carmelita's warm mound as several other hands groped his raging cock.

"Let's take this to your room," Tina said.

Things got hot and steamy inside the elevator. Carmelita and Sokda were exchanging frantic, libidinous kisses while Tina got on her knees in front of Pete, nuzzling his hard dick through his shorts. Before they reached the third floor, she had slipped her hand inside and taken a firm grip on his pulsating shaft.

The door to his room had scarcely opened when Carmelita wiggled out of her top, cupping her firm breast in both hands. She offered Pete both of her stiffened nipples to take into his mouth. He happily obliged, taking one firmly between his lips, then the other one. Carmelita shuddered as he sucked and kneaded her soft flesh. A pair of hands traveled up his bare thighs, pausing at his zipper. After a couple of tugs, Pete's fly fell open. Next thing he knew, his shorts and boxers were around his ankles.

The tip of his dick suddenly entered something warm and moist. When Pete glanced down, Tina's head was bobbing back and forth as she sucked his dick. He turned back to finish what he had started with Carmelita's titties. They were so responsive to every flick of his tongue.

"You can cum in my mouth if you want, baby," Tina moaned, continuing to suck his cock.

As his sensitive glans disappeared into her mouth, Pete felt another set of lips sucking on his balls. Sokda's mouth felt so good that he was about to explode. Carmelita pulled him toward the bed, and all three girls stopped long enough to remove their skimpy bikinis and join Pete on the California-king-sized bed. They shoved him roughly onto his back. He lay there admiring the beauty that stood there before him. Tina's hot lips once again encircled his dick, and Carmelita squatted over his face. She placed her fingers over her moist lips, spreading them for his tongue to enter.

"Let me taste that pussy, baby," Pete said, eagerly licking her slit and driving his tongue between her labia.

She ground her pussy into his mouth, groaning and biting her bottom lip. Pete wrapped his lips around her swollen clitoris, sucking it softly. Carmelita was lost in her own emotions, rubbing back and forth over his face. Tina had his dick so deep in her mouth that, she occasionally had to keep stopping from gagging on it. Her nose kept hitting his pubic bone every time she took him into her warm mouth. She cupped his balls with both hands because she knew that he would soon be shooting his creamy load down her throat.

Carmelita was craving Sokda's pretty pussy in her mouth as she watched her fingering herself. She signaled her over so she could try it out. The bed shook as she straddled over Pete's head, waiting to receive Carmelita's warm tongue. Carmelita was the first to get her orgasm. Her cries of ecstasy were muffled by Sokda's cunt, but unmistakable. This escapade was driving Pete over the edge, and Tina must have recognized it, because she removed his dick from her mouth, wrapping her fingers around its base. She jerked it until he ejaculated all over her hands and face. Pete felt like he was in heaven, but it wasn't over yet.

"I have to feel your dick inside of me right now," Carmelita said, suddenly scooting backward, pulling away from his mouth.

He could feel Tina's hand repositioning his dick, then Carmelita's sexy body flopping down on it. Her pussy was wet and warm as her walls clamped around his shaft. Pete threw his head back on the pillow and closed his eyes. He could feel his balls aching to release another load, but it seemed like she was holding him back. Carmelita pumped up and down like a madwoman, and he rammed his hips upward as Tina began squeezing his scrotum.

"Oh shit, don't stop. That dick feels so good," Carmelita screamed out in pleasure.

"Oh, you like that, don't you?" he replied, gripping her waist.

"Yessssss," was all she could get out before having another orgasm.

Sokda took up Carmelita's place over Pete's mouth and began to suck on her nipples. As her delectable pussy lips settled over his tongue, Pete reached upward and found her breasts. He tweaked them while driving his tongue into her hole. Sokda's juices poured out over his face, and like a vacuum cleaner, he sucked it all up as he continued to stroke Carmelita's pussy.

In spite of Tina's fingers clamped around his balls, Pete was seconds from a colossal orgasm. He was almost screaming, but Sokda's pussy had sealed itself over his mouth. When Tina released her grip, he exploded into Carmelita's pussy, still pounding away as her eyes rolled into the back of her head. His balls slapped up at her crotch even as Tina tried to suck up both of their juices.

"Mmmmmmm, it tastes like strawberries," Tina replied, licking her lips.

"Oh my God, I'm about to cum, baby," Carmelita screamed out.

She stiffened and shuddered, her knees tight against his sides. She sat down hard, impaled on the whole length of his spurting dick, coming like crazy. At that same moment, Sokda cried out and came, almost shaking herself off Pete's avidly sucking mouth. Carmelita pushed herself off his slightly limp penis and plunged it into her mouth.

She flicked the tip with her tongue, trying to suck up the remainder of the semen Tina had left. In no time, his dick was hard and ready to go again. One last lash of her tongue, and it was replaced with Tina's pink pussy. Pete could tell that she was close to an orgasm by the way she was riding his shaft.

"That's it. Just like that, baby. It's so big, I can feel it in my stomach," she said working her muscles with wicked precision. "Faster, harder, oh shit, yes."

Seconds later she burst into an impassioned cry that intertwined with Sokda's as he brought her to another climax with his tongue. He pulled Sokda down as Tina rolled off of him, and sat her on his still throbbing dick.

"Yes, baby, you're next to take this ride," Pete moaned, bouncing Sokda up and down until they both came in yet another great explosion then collapsed on the bed exhausted.

They all fell asleep on the bed, until Carmelita woke up in the middle of the night to use the bathroom. She grabbed her purse and walked into the bathroom, closing the door behind her. She sat on the toilet, then opened her purse, pulling out a mini camera. As she checked the contents, a smile brushed across her face. She quickly placed the camera back into her purse, then wiped herself and flushed the toilet. She quietly woke her friends so they could get out of there before Pete woke up.

When she went to pick up her bikini bottoms off the floor, she noticed something shiny sticking out of his pants pocket. Curiosity got the best of her, and she looked inside, finding his badge, and his gun holster was tucked underneath.

"Oh shit, he's a cop," she whispered to herself.

Carmelita thought that they just messed up, until she remembered what she overheard her boss saying in his office. That's when she realized that it was all going to come together after all. She checked her cell phone, noticing that she had three missed calls from her husband. She decided to call him back when they were on the road. She had told him that she was going to hang out with her friends and that she would be home late.

They all got dressed and exited the hotel without waking Pete. When he woke up, the beautiful women were gone. He took a quick shower, then hit the road back home. He had some affairs he needed to get in order, and he still had a job to do until the transition into his new one was put in motion. He made a call as soon as he got on the PA Turnpike to the office.

"What's up, partner? Are you coming in today?" Det. Wilbur said on the receiving end of the phone. She became his new partner when his old one was killed in the line of duty. She had been on the force for five years, and a detective for two.

She was married to a beautiful woman name Ariel. Ariel was from Mexico and came over to the US as an illegal immigrant. She needed a green card so she could become a citizen, and Megan had helped her out. Megan was bisexual and fell in love with Ariel after a night of steamy sex. The two eloped, then Ariel moved in with her, and they'd been together ever since.

"I'm on my way back now. The meeting went extremely well, and I should be taking over very soon," Det. Davis stated confidently.

"That's good. Then I will have a friend in high places for real," Det. Wilbur joked.

She was wondering how they were going to skip over the captains and other people with higher ranks, to make Det. Davis the new DPC. But she brushed it off as just being in the right place at the right time. Megan filled him in on everything that had taken place while he was gone, and then they conversed for a few more minutes before ending the call. He called his wife and talked to her briefly, then turned up the music, put on the cruise control, and enjoyed his ride back.

* * *

"So did you have fun with your friends last night?" Boris asked, giving his wife a kiss on the lips that she used on someone else's penis last night.

"Yeah, we went to a banquet. It was a lot of business executives there, so I had a chance to meet different people in politics, and I'm really glad I took this job," Carmelita said, kicking off her shoes.

"You better hurry up if you plan on getting to work on time."

"I just have to change my clothes and put on my makeup," she said, rushing upstairs.

She removed the camera from her purse, then opened her hidden safe that was behind the painting and placed it inside. After locking it up, she got dressed and headed to work with a smile on her face. Her plan was coming along very well, and soon she would have everyone eating out of her hand.

"Glad you can join us," Morgan stated as soon as Carmelita stepped off the elevator. "Hurry up because we have a lot of things on my agenda to discuss."

She didn't respond to his comment; she just rushed to her desk, removed her tablet, and followed him to his office for a briefing on the day's events. Even though she was typing everything the governor was saying onto her tablet, she was still reminiscing about what she and her friends did last night and how she was going to use the tapes to blackmail the people on them. She had been secretly recording different people for the last month. At first it was just for her own amusement; then it became clear that she should hold on to them for some kind of leverage.

"That will be all for now. Let me know when my eleven o'clock gets here, and I want to get together later to talk about your tardiness," Morgan stated, snapping Carmelita out of her daydream.

"Yes, Mr. Governor," she replied, heading out of the conference room.

She spent the rest of the day taking care of all the phone calls and doing paperwork for her boss. Morgan left before he had the chance to talk to her, so she clocked out and went home. On her way she called her husband, but he was at work. Boris was the general manager of a club called Vanity Grand. It was located in Southwest Philly, off of Passyunk Ave. She was familiar with the type of club it was because that's where they first met four years ago.

"Are you going to be there all night, or just until later?"

"I'm not sure, but I will call you later on to let you know. Are you gonna cook tonight or order takeout?" Boris asked.

"Whatever you want," she replied in that seductive tone that always drove him crazy. She had a way of turning him on no matter how far apart they were. The chemistry they shared only intensified each day. Maybe it had something to do with them both living double lives, with multiple partners.

"Surprise me. Love you," he said, ending the call.

Carmelita went home, took a hot shower, then fell asleep on the bed with just her towel wrapped around her. She was too tired to do anything else.

* * *

Sahmeer's wounds were healing quite well in the short period of time he'd been released from the hospital. He had a nurse that would come over to give him physical therapy twice a week. She was from the University of Pennsylvania, had been his father's trainer when he was injured, and was drop-dead gorgeous. Sahmeer would stare at her constantly, but that was as far as it would go. His wife meant the world to him, and he wasn't going to let anything jeopardize that, especially after what happened with his father.

"You are truly showing signs of improvement, sir. I'm guessing that you won't need me too much longer," the nurse said, rubbing Sahmeer's leg before they worked it out on the treadmill.

"My dad is 'sir.' Call me Sahmeer, and I'm still going to need your assistance for my rehabilitation process. It may seem like I'm getting better, but my leg begs to differ."

"Okay, great. Let's get to work then," she replied, helping him up.

Sahmeer got on the treadmill and waited for her to adjust the settings. She set the timer, then hit the start button, and he began his workout. She monitored his movements from her laptop to make sure his heartbeat stayed at a reasonable pace. They continued his therapy for two hours before she thought he had enough. She was right: he had definitely improved a lot. He was moving around easily now.

"I will see you Wednesday, Sahmeer," Lorena said, packing her equipment up.

"Akiylah will be here in a minute. She was having a back spasm and wanted you to check it out if you have time."

"Okay, I can do that."

"I'm going to take a shower, but you can fix yourself a drink if you want. You know where everything is. Let me know if you need anything," he replied, heading out the door.

Lorena poured herself a drink and waited for Akiylah to come. Lorena had a schoolgirl crush on her because of her caramel complexion. Lorena was Spanish and African American, with a petite body. She had short black hair, long sexy legs that men could never get enough of, and 38DD breasts. Akiylah walked in wearing a tennis skirt and a Polo Ralph Lauren T-shirt. She sat her purse down on the table and walked over to where Lorena was sitting.

"Hey, your husband told me about your back spasms. Would you be interested in a massage?" Lorena asked, sitting her drink down.

Akiylah shrugged her shoulders. "Why not? Maybe it will help my back."

Akiylah went into the other room and got butt naked, hanging her clothes on one of the hooks. She slipped on one of the silk robes from the cabinet and walked back out as Lorena was setting up her table. She placed a large soft towel over the padded table that was now sitting in the middle of the room. Akiylah walked over and lay down, closing her eyes.

The warmth of the lights and the aroma of the scented water evaporating over the stones was calming and relaxing. She let her mind drift to another place, trying to get it off the pain that was running through her back. She sighed deeply as Lorena chopped her calves, massaged her ankles, and worked her way up to Akiylah's back. The pain settled down and turned into pleasure. Lorena moved up to the top of the table and slid Akiylah's robe down until it covered her feet. Akiylah got lost in her own thoughts as Lorena rubbed some hot oil into her shoulders and down her arms to the small of her back. The moans that slipped from her lips caught her by surprise.

Lorena was working her ass, and the spot between her thighs was slippery and throbbing. Bit by bit, Akiylah found herself rotating her hips as Lorena squeezed and palmed her cheeks. Akiylah's pussy was so soaked, it felt like Lorena had poured some of the hot oil down the crack of her ass. She squeezed her thighs together and ground her pussy into the table, shivering and moaning out loud. Akiylah felt Lorena nudge her legs open slightly, and when she slid two fingers into her wet pussy from behind, she didn't even try to stop her.

"Oh God," she moaned as Lorena pressed down on her lower spine with one hand and rubbed her swollen clit and played in her pussy with the other.

Akiylah was amazed when she felt Lorena's hot breath on her ass. Lorena's lips were wet on her ass, and she yelped when she spread her pussy lips apart, sticking her tongue into Akiylah's hole. She was turned on even more now, whimpering like a baby as she felt herself about to cum. It was then that she finally realized that what she was doing was wrong. She jumped up and grabbed her clothes, rushing out of the room. She loved the way it felt, but with everything that was going on, it wasn't the right time for it.

Lorena smiled at the way she ran out. She had finally gotten the chance to taste her goodies. She sat down in the chair and played with her pussy until she exploded all over her fingers. The whole time, she was thinking about her encounter with Akiylah. She couldn't wait to get another chance at her. It was her first time, but not the last.

SIX

KEVIN WOKE UP TO the sound of his cell phone ringing. He looked at the screen and jumped up before answering it.

"Hello," he said, wiping his eyes.

"Where you at, bro? You're late for practice, and you know we have a very hard game tonight," Marcus replied on the other end.

"I slept late, but I'm on my way right now. Give me about a half hour."

"Kev, just hurry up and get here, man. Coach is pissed off right now. I'll tell him you're stuck in traffic or something," Marcus told him, ending the call.

Kevin sat his phone back on the nightstand, then noticed the white bag of powder sitting there. He felt someone moving behind him and turned around, only to see a beautiful naked female lying in the bed asleep. That's when he realized what had happened last night. He was in a hotel room after picking some chick up from somewhere.

"Shit, I am really tripping right now," he said to himself, rushing to the bathroom to take a quick shower.

By the time he got out and came back in the room, the woman was sitting on the bed dressed, snorting a line of coke. She looked up and smiled at him as he threw on his clothes. He thought for a minute but still couldn't remember where he picked her up from.

"Come get some of this, baby, before we leave," she said, holding the straw out to him.

"No, I have practice, and I'm already late. Call yourself a cab to take you home, and I'll see you later," he said, passing her two hundred dollars from his wallet, then rushing out the door.

When Kevin arrived at the arena for practice, everyone had already started. The coach looked at him like he wanted to strangle him. He blew his whistle signaling for everyone to stop.

"Practice some pick and roll plays, and I'll be back," he told his assistant coaches. "Kevin, I need to speak with you in my office now."

"Don't let him look in your eyes," Marcus said, knowing what Kevin had taken.

"I only had a little last night to calm my nerves," Kevin whispered to him.

"It doesn't matter how much you had. I told you to leave that shit alone. You have too much going on for you right now to just throw it away for some fucking drugs," Marcus replied, getting angry.

"I said, my office," the coach yelled out before the two of them got into a heated argument.

Kevin walked away to talk with his coach, leaving Marcus standing there heated.

Coach O'Brian held the door open for Kevin, and as soon as his feet crossed the threshold, he slammed it shut, causing everybody to look in that direction. "Sit your ass down," he said, pointing to a chair. Kevin sat down, waiting for his coach to let him have it.

"Coach, let me explain," he began saying, but was cut off.

"I don't want to hear it, Kevin. You are one of my vets, and what you do reflects on everyone else in that locker room. I put my name on the line for you and Marcus to keep y'all here, and this is how you repay me?"

"Coach, I'm truly sorry, and it will never happen again. I will be here an hour early for the rest of the season, I promise."

"You will not be starting tonight, and after the game, I want a hundred suicides. You will also take a drug test before you leave here today. Did you think for one moment that I wouldn't notice your dilated eyes? Now get the hell out there and get ready for the game tonight before you really piss me off," he said, heading toward the door.

Kevin walked back into the gym ready to work. He was a bit out of sync, but by the end of practice, he came around. Marcus stayed with the rest of the team, doing the suicides together to let their coach know that no matter what, they were a team and they stuck together.

"I know what you're thinking, and I promise that if I get through this, I'm done with that stuff," Kevin stated as he and Marcus headed toward their cars.

"Meet me at my home to go over some film," Marcus said to Kevin.

"I'm right behind you," Kevin replied, hopping into his car and pulling off.

He needed a hit right now but didn't want to risk it. He was already in hot water if his piss test came back positive. When he was told that he had to take a urine test, he went to his locker and took out the vial of urine he kept there for emergencies like that. Now he was just waiting for the results to come back.

* * *

"Have you heard anything from your husband or his attorneys?" Raphael asked as he and Carla lay back in bed watching *Empire* on the television.

"They were supposed to contact my lawyer today, but she hasn't said anything as of yet," she said, rubbing his chest.

"Maybe you should give them a call."

"I will tomorrow if I don't hear anything by then," she replied getting up to use the bathroom. While Carla was in the bathroom, the doorbell rang.

Raphael sat up looking around for his pants on the floor. He slipped them on just in time, as the bell rang again. Carla came out and picked up her panties from the floor.

"Are you expecting someone?" she asked, slipping them on, then grabbing her dress.

"No, but I'm going to see who it is now."

Raphael walked out of the room to see who was so impatient. When he opened the door, standing there before him was his ex-wife. What really had his attention was the little boy that was with her. He had a very close resemblance to someone he knew. Himself!

"What are you doing here?" he asked, stepping out and closing the door behind him.

"Is that all you have to say? I came all the way from Atlanta to let him meet his father and you're not even going to invite us in?" she said with a smirk on her face.

"Wait a minute, that's my son?" She nodded her head up and down. "So why am I just now hearing about this?"

"Maybe if you would have answered your phone or the text I sent you, you would have known."

"I thought you were trying to start some more trouble. Our marriage was doomed from the beginning, if you didn't notice," Raphael replied.

"I was hoping that we could maybe start all over for the sake of our child."

"I don't even know if he's really mine yet. We have to set up a paternity test, and even if it comes back saying that he's mine, we will never be together again."

Carla opened the door, fully dressed, and looked at the three of them. She had heard a little bit of their conversation and didn't want to interfere.

"I hope I'm not interrupting anything, but I have to go meet with my lawyer. She just called asking me to come to the office immediately," Carla said, easing past them.

"Is everything okay? Do you need me to go with you?" Raphael said, concerned.

"No, everything is okay. I'll just give you a call later."

"I'm going with you. Give me a second to grab my keys." He turned to Elaina. "Is there anything else you need to talk about?"

"We don't have anywhere to go. My boyfriend was putting his hands on me, and I couldn't take it anymore, so I packed some of our stuff and left," she told him.

If it was anything he hated, it was a man putting his hands on a female. He turned toward Carla and gave her a look of concern. She already knew what he wanted to say. Since they had been seeing each other, Carla had moved in with him, and they had become an item.

"Why don't you let them stay in the guest room until they find a place of their own," Carla suggested, shocking both Raphael and Elaina.

"Are you sure?" Elaina asked, looking at Carla.

"Yes, I'm sure. Look at that handsome face right there. What is your name?" she said, bending down and squeezing the little boy's cheeks.

"Christopher."

"Well, it's nice to meet you, Chris. Would you like some cookies and milk?" He nodded his head up and down excitedly. "Come on, I'll get them for him while you help her take the bags up to their room," she told Raphael.

"Thank you," Elaina mouthed to Carla as she took Christopher inside to get a snack. Raphael helped her take her bags inside and up to her room. After doing that, he and Carla left out to meet with Carla's lawyer. Morgan and his lawyers had all reached an agreement that would benefit both parties. She had to sign the paperwork that would finalize the deal.

"We'll talk about this later," Carla said, knowing that he was thinking about what happened a few minutes ago with his ex-wife.

"Okay," was all he could get out.

They pulled up to the attorney's office just as Morgan was getting out of his limo. He watched as they exited the car, Carla walking past him with a smirk on her face. He noticed how they held hands, and just a pinch of jealousy came over him. He still loved her after all the bullshit he put her through, but now it was over. He even wondered sometimes what his old fling Symira was up to. "Can we hurry up and get this over with, because I need to get back to Harrisburg. My lawyers and yours have already made an agreement that we both agreed to, so you sign, and I'll do the same, and our business is over," Morgan said to Carla.

"I didn't cheat on you. It was the other way around, so don't you dare talk to me like that again. I hope I never see your face again. How can you live with yourself knowing what you've done?" she replied, signing the papers.

"We're not here for this, so can we get this over with?" one of Morgan's lawyers asked.

"He's right, Carla. Don't let him get to you," her attorney whispered in her ear.

After it was all said and done, Carla walked out of there richer than she had ever been. The settlement gave her the house in Philadelphia, and an alimony check every month. She already had the house on the market to be sold because she didn't want to stay there anymore. She was happy with being at Raphael's home. They went shopping so Carla could cook dinner for their guests. Then they headed home to get the long-awaited confrontation over with. Raphael just wondered why his girlfriend would suggest that his ex-wife stay with them. But there was a method to her madness, and she would reveal it when she was ready.

* * *

Symira had finally made it back to her doctor's office for another sonogram, and was watching the monitor as her doctor explained what was going on. Her breathing was heavy from anticipation, and she was getting nervous by the second thinking something was wrong with the baby.

"Well it seems like there may be a problem with your fetus, Symira."

"Wait a minute. What are you saying?" Symira replied, looking at her doctor with fear in her eyes. She wanted to sit up, but he held her where she was.

"Don't get up yet. I have to tell you the news first. I had to make sure that I was right before I mentioned it to you," he said, looking at the screen.

"What is it that you're telling me? And don't bullshit me."

"You have more than one fetus growing inside of you. Symira, you are having twins, my dear. Congratulations," he said, smiling.

Symira couldn't believe her ears. She was having twins, and the sad part about it was she still didn't know who the father was. That was something that she needed to know before deciding her next move. She was excited and decided to go buy herself something. Once she left the doctor's office, she headed over to her best friend's car lot to see if her car was ready. She had already given him half the money for it, and she was hoping it was done.

When she got to the shop, everyone was sitting around as if there wasn't anything to do. Symira walked over to the desk to ask for Josh, who was the manager. Every time she came there, all the workers would try to flirt with her. Maybe it had something to do with the short skirts or the tight-fitting jeans she would always wear, but she really enjoyed it.

"Good afternoon, guys. Is Josh still here?"

"He's in the back in his office," one of the fellas said. "When are you going to let me take you out again?"

Malik and Symira had gone on a double date before with Josh and his wife, but she wasn't feeling him like that. They thought it would be a good idea, to help her get over her previous relationship, but it ended up being a disaster. She had to pay for dinner because he didn't have his wallet. Come to find out, he didn't have any money period.

"When you become a real man and stop trying to manipulate other people. Stop trying to act like you have money but you're really broke. You can't afford me anyway," she replied, degrading his ego in front of his boys.

They all started laughing at him as she headed to the back. Knowing that they were staring at her ass, she gave them a show by switching harder as she entered Josh's office. He was on the phone talking to his wife.

"Give me a second, I'm talking to Megan," he stated, motioning for Symira to have a seat.

"Okay, tell her I said hi," she replied, walking over to one of the chairs.

He was saying something to his wife when Symira sat down. As she crossed her legs, he stared right at her goodies. He just shook his head at her.

"Symira is here to pick up her car keys. She said 'hi.' Let me give you a call back," he said into the receiver. He smiled then said, "Okay, love you too."

He put the phone down and got out of his chair to retrieve her keys. Symira picked up a magazine and started looking through it. Josh took her keys out of the lockbox and passed them to her.

"She still thinks that we used to hook up or something. She always wondered why we are so close," Josh said, standing by the edge of his desk.

"She will always think that. If I wanted you, I could have had you."

"Is that right?" he said, folding his arms.

Symira wanted to test his willpower to see if he really did want to get in between her legs. Being pregnant had her hormones racing, so she was always horny. She needed dick 24/7, and since she was single, she would take it from whoever she could get it from. Her stomach still was flat, so nobody knew she was expecting a baby. She stood up and walked over to where he was standing.

"I always saw how you stared at me when I was with your cousin when we were little. I think that's why we became good friends in high school. You wouldn't let anything happen to me," she said, pushing him away from the desk. She sat up on it, her skirt so short you could see the black lace panties underneath.

"That was because you were a hothead always getting into shit," he chuckled devilishly, trying not to stare.

She caught his eyes and noticed the bulge that was forming in the slacks he had on. Symira leaned back on the desk and spread her legs seductively.

"Lock the door and come here for a minute."

Josh thought about Megan momentarily, but the head between his legs erased that thought. He had to admit that he wanted to try her one time; his wife wouldn't know. He locked his office door and joined her, hoping he would finally get that chance.

Symira stuck one finger in her pussy and then lifted her finger to his lips.

"Come taste me," she said as she licked her sweet lips.

Josh licked the wetness off her fingers while grinding his hardness against her body. His hands sent a slight tingle up her spine.

"Hmmm," he moaned, nibbling gently on her neck.

He knelt down on one knee, moving her panties to the side and slipping his tongue into her pussy, twirling it in circles inside of her. She moaned so loudly that she was sure the entire establishment heard her, but it didn't deter their session one bit. This was one of the best head games she had ever had. He inserted two fingers into her opening as his tongue played with her clitoris. Symira grabbed his head, moving her hips like a dancer to his tongue, which moved like a snake. She started pressing her vagina firmly against his mouth. It felt so good that she couldn't help but to have a quick orgasm. Josh put his hands underneath her skirt until both of them gripped her ass cheeks. He massaged them as he helped her grind her pussy on his tongue. He reached down with one hand and started stroking himself to bring his man to full erection.

She looked down and watched him pleasing himself, and the pleasurable look on his face brought her to another climax. Seconds later he grunted loudly, also erupting all over the floor. Symira wanted to fuck now, so she started rubbing his dick, bringing it back to life. Once he was hard again, he stood up, positioning his dick at her opening. He was just about to enter, when she placed a hand on his chest, halting him.

"Do you have a condom?"

"No, we don't need one. I know how to pull out. I won't cum inside you," Josh said softly.

"That is not an option, baby. You know what the saying is: no glove, no love." She sighed, standing up and fixing her skirt.

"Come on, Symira, just let me stick the head in," he said flirtatiously, still stroking his dick.

As tempted as she was right now, she didn't want to make that mistake. She smiled at him and headed for the door. Before walking out, she turned around and said, "Maybe we can do this another time. Your wife would be mad if we did this without her. See if you can talk her into it, and let me know."

She walked out, leaving him with blue balls. Josh's workers watched as she strolled out of there with a smirk on her face. They already had an idea of what happened from the muffled sounds they heard coming from his office.

"See you later, sexy," Malik said, disappointed that he didn't get any play.

SEVEN

PETE AND HIS FAMILY were sitting around watching the presidential election on television. This was a monumental moment for two reasons. The first was, this could possibly be the first woman president ever, and the second was, the reigns may be given to someone who never had political or military experience before. It was 2:30 a.m., and the votes were now in. The people of the United States had spoken, and Donald Trump was now the new president elect.

"No one seen this coming, but that's what happens when a high percentage of people doesn't vote," Pete's wife said, sitting next to her husband and daughters.

"Maybe it's because no one appreciated the fact that Hillary lied about those emails, or that they just don't trust women to have so much power," Veronica replied.

"Regardless of any of that, we have to give him the chance to succeed or go down in a disastrous way. Whether we like it or not, he will be running this country for at least the next four years," Pete told his daughter.

"Well I think we are in trouble. What's going to happen to all those people that came here to get away from those communist states?"

"I'm sure he will deal with it accordingly. Like I said, give the man a chance," Pete stated, turning off the television. "It's late, I'm going to bed."

"I'll be right behind you," his wife told him.

Pete and Iris had been together for eighteen years, and married for ten. They met when he was a rookie on the police force. She gave up work to raise their two kids, Veronica (eighteen) and Linda (seven). She missed being an emergency dispatcher and was hoping to go back to work someday. At the age of thirty-eight, Veronica wasn't getting any younger and was at the peak of her sexuality. Her husband was never around, so most of her days were spent alone with her youngest daughter, and lonely. She and her husband had only had sex twice in the last two months, and that was only a brief encounter.

"Okay, sweetie, it's time for bed," she said to Linda.

"Do I have to go to school tomorrow, Mommy?"

"Yes, that's why you have to get to bed. You only have a few hours left to sleep, so goodnight," Iris said, giving her a kiss.

"Come on, I'll tuck you in," Veronica offered.

Iris's children headed upstairs to get ready for bed. She grabbed a bottle of wine and two glasses, then headed upstairs also. Tonight she wanted to have some alone time with her husband. When she entered the bedroom, Pete quickly hung up the phone.

"Drink?" she asked, holding up the bottle.

He shook his head no, then started getting dressed. Iris knew that meant that he was about to go back to work, and once again leave her alone. She threw the bottle on the floor, causing Pete to jump.

"What's wrong with you?"

"I wanted to spend time with my husband, that's what's wrong with me. We haven't been intimate in weeks, and now you're leaving again," she whined.

"Iris, there has been a murder over this election bullshit. I have to go. It's my job."

She knew she was being selfish, so she calmed down. Pete walked over and kneeled down in front of her. He grabbed her hand and rubbed it gently.

"I promise after this is all over with, I'll take you on a romantic date anywhere you like," he told her.

Before she could respond, he got up, kissed her softly on the lips, and left. Iris sat at the edge of their bed contemplating her next move. She was beautiful and couldn't figure out why her husband wasn't sexually attracted to her. Even though she was thirty-eight, she looked more like she was twenty-eight, with the body of a goddess. The only conclusion that she could muster up was that he was having an affair. Her stomach churned at the thought, but it was something she had to take into consideration. The thought of revenge suddenly crossed her mind.

* * *

"Hello, are you coming?"

"Yes, I just left out the house. Where do you want to meet?" he said into the Bluetooth headset.

"Come to the Marriott downtown on Market Street. My room number is 1305," the voice on the other end replied.

"Okay, I'll be there in about thirty minutes."

"See you then!"

Pete ended the call, then turned on his favorite song while hitting the gas pedal, accelerating his speed to ninety miles per hour. He was thinking about how this election may have just worked out in his favor. Now he was sure that his homicide detective days would soon be up and that he would be filling that DPC spot.

It only took him about twenty minutes to arrive at the hotel. If he had told his wife that he was going to a meeting, she would have looked at him like he was crazy. There was no way someone would be at a meeting at three o'clock in the morning. He parked in the garage, then took the elevator to the thirteenth floor.

The sound of someone knocking at the door caused Sodka to exit the shower before she was done. She threw on a robe and headed toward the door.

"You got here earlier than you said," she said, moving to the side to let him in.

"Traffic was clear," he replied, gripping her around the waist.

They both fell to the floor, and Pete stuck his tongue into her mouth. He untied her robe, letting it fall from her shoulders, then licked each nipple, causing her to moan. Pete continued licking down her body until he reached her pussy. As he began sucking on her clit, she started to jerk from the orgasm that was forming.

"Oh my," she screamed out in pleasure from her juices flowing from his mouth, down the crack of her ass.

She was dying to get him undressed. She unbuttoned his shirt and pulled it off of him, revealing his athletic body. Being a cop, he stayed in the gym so he wouldn't end up like most of his potbellied friends on the force. Sodka ran her hands over the bulge in his pants, becoming even more excited, especially between her legs.

It didn't take her long to get his pants off and his brick-hard shaft into her watery mouth. It was swollen with anticipation. She tasted the tip with her tongue, then engulfed the head back into her hungry mouth.

"It still tastes so good," she mumbled.

"Yeah, your mouth still feels . . . Oh shit," he yelled, not being able to finish his statement because her tongue ring was sending shockwaves throughout his body.

Before she knew it, he was holding her hair and his dick was inside her mouth up to his balls. She sucked him hard until she felt him stiffening up. Thinking he was ready to cum, she stopped sucking and got on all fours, waiting for him to hurry up and slide into her pussy from behind. In seconds he slipped a condom on and was thrusting hard into her as she worked the muscles in her vagina. He pulled almost all the way out on each stroke, then rammed himself back into her, causing her to scream out in pain.

When he reached around to stimulate her clitoris with his fingers, it wasn't long before they both were cumming explosively. Sodka felt his warm cream on her back and ass as he pulled out, removed the condom, and released his semen all over her. They fucked until the wee hours of the morning, until Pete had to leave.

"I hope we'll get the chance to do this again. This was better than our little rendezvous we had in Harrisburg. How long will you be here in Philly?" Pete asked.

"I live here. That's why I called you. You didn't think I came all the way out here just to see you? I mean, the dick is good, but not that good," she joked.

"Don't flatter yourself, sweetie. I have a wife at home."

"So why are you here?"

"Because," he said, rubbing on her pussy, "I enjoy doing this."

Sodka started breathing hard, closing her eyes enjoying his touch. Her kitty became moist all over again, then it stopped. She opened her eyes when she felt him move his hand away. He could see her juices running down her legs.

"So you just gonna leave me like this?" she said, inserting two fingers inside her vagina. It made squishy noises as she pumped in and out.

"Sorry, but I have work to do," Pete replied, leaving the room.

Sodka stopped as soon as the door shut, and grabbed her cell phone out of her purse to make a call. After three rings, someone picked up on the other end.

"It's done." She smiled.

"Good," was all the the person said before hanging up.

* * *

Kevin was tired of being in a big house with no one to share it with. Against his son's disapproval, he decided to put it up for sale. He and Carla were using the same realtor because she was the best at what she did. She already had scheduled for someone to look at it today. They would be there within the hour, so he was making sure that everything was in order.

Marcus was even wondering why he was selling the house after they'd been around each other so long. He told him that it had something to do with the memories of his wife, and her not being there, and that he still lived with it every day. Marcus had the feeling that he was holding back, though. He didn't press the issue because it was a sensitive matter. The cleaning crew was pulling out just as a car was pulling into the driveway.

"Kevin, they're here," the realtor said excitedly.

"Here I come now," he replied, walking down the steps. "Is everything ready?"

"It is. The cleaning crew finished just in time," she told him as they waited for the potential buyers to exit the car.

Kevin's eyes lit up at the two beautiful women that stepped out of the car. They looked like twins that came straight off the runway.

"Good afternoon, ladies! I'm Sarah, the one you talked to on the phone. This is the owner, Kevin Green."

"It's nice to meet both of you. I'm Jade, and this is my sister, Brittney," the taller of the two said, shaking their hands politely.

Her sister shook their hands also. She gave Kevin a seductive smile that almost drove him crazy.

"Well let me show you around," Sarah said, escorting them all inside to look around. Kevin played the back while she did her thing.

The house basically sold itself. Once they saw the pool out back and the humongous bedrooms, they were sold. Kevin couldn't help but wonder if their rich husbands were paying for all this or if it was part of a settlement from a divorce or something like that. The jury was still out on that verdict. They talked for a while, and he found out that only Brittney was married. Jade was the CEO of a charter school that was built by Bill Gates in West Philly. He had only invested the money, but she was the brains behind it all.

Kevin couldn't believe that she was so independent. Her sister had money also. Jade had invested in some stock and cashed out at the right time by selling it when it was at an all-time high. Together they were a force to be reckoned with, and you could tell that by the way they carried themselves.

"I'm sold on this. How about you, Sis?" Brittany said.

"I think our mother will love this. It's definitely the right choice," Jade concluded.

"So this is for your mother?" Kevin questioned, disappointed.

"It's actually for all of us. We always promised our mother a big house in a gated community, and we want to keep that promise. She has cancer in her stomach, so we want to make sure she has everything she needs," Brittany stated sadly.

"Sorry to hear that," Kevin told her sincerely.

"Thank you! So when can we sign the paperwork?"

"If you like, we can head back to my office and take care of that now," Sarah said.

"So you're fine with the asking price?" Kevin asked.

"I'm fine with it," Jade said proudly.

She wanted to show him that money didn't mean anything when it came to their mother's happiness. She gave up her last to raise them, and they would do the same.

"Okay, let's go then. Kevin, I will give you a call later to fill you in on all the particulars," Sarah said, walking toward her car.

"It was nice doing business with you, Kevin. Hopefully I'll see you again," Jade said, shaking his hand.

"That can be arranged," Kevin replied flirtatiously.

"Set it up and give me a call," she told him, walking away.

He stood there watching as they pulled off, then thought about what he had just done. He sold his $1.5 million home for $1.8 million. The problem was he still hadn't told his best friend that he requested to be traded and management had granted that wish. He was now a Golden State Warrior.

They needed a defensive player and called Philadelphia about him. Now that he had sold his home, it was inevitable that he tell everyone. Even Mike didn't know what was going down yet. All he knew was that his dad was selling the house.

Everyone would soon find out when they turned on the television, because it was breaking news on every sports channel. Marcus already knew because he saw it on TMZ Sports last night and his agent told him. They had the same sports agent ever since they were in college. Marcus was just waiting to see how long it was going to take Kevin to say something.

"Mike, I need you to meet me over at Marcus's house. Where are you right now?" Kevin said, facetiming his son.

"I'm actually a few minutes away. What's wrong, Pops?"

"You'll see when you get there. We'll be waiting for you. I want to tell everybody at one time."

Once everyone was together, Kevin explained what was going on. They all realized the fact that he was moving on, and gave him their blessing. Mike decided that he was going to stay in Philly and get his own place. Marcus told him that he could stay with them until he got it, and he accepted the offer. Kevin wished Michelle was still here to take this journey with him. She might have been gone, but she would never be forgotten. Her legacy would live on in his heart.

EIGHT

SASHA HAD TAKEN A trip with Akiylah back to the Virgin Islands to see her mom, who was sick. They were only supposed to be gone for a few days. Sasha didn't want to leave Sahmeer, but he insisted that she go and treat it as if she were on vacation. Akiylah showed her where Sahmeer was when he had his accident, and she was surprised because the water was so beautiful. There wasn't a shark in sight anywhere.

They made Caribbean food, which Sasha really enjoyed, and Akiylah's sisters showed Sasha how to dance like them. She felt like she was twenty-one all over again twerking and winding. Today made all the adversities that she and her family went through seem worth it, because she realized how much they meant to her.

She hoped that it would still be this way when she told Sahmeer who his real father was. She didn't know how much longer she would be able to avoid the inevitable. He had to know the truth, so she told herself that she would tell him as soon as she returned home. Right now she was going to enjoy the water.

"I wish I could stay here forever," Sasha said to Akiylah's sister.

"Me wish me could go to the States for a while. Want to switch?" She smiled.

Vanessa wanted to experience what it would be like in the United States. She had never been there before, and hearing her sister talk about it only piqued her interest even more.

"How about you come visit us whenever you can. You're family now, and you can bring your mom if she wants to come. I'm going to take a swim in this beautiful water," Sasha said, dropping her towel and running toward the crystal-clear sea.

Vanessa dropped her towel and followed her. The water was nice and cool covering their skin. Sasha never knew that she would enjoy this so much. It was actually what she needed at the moment. Akiylah came out to join them in their water. After swimming for a while, they went inside to check on their mother.

"Sasha, are you enjoying yourself?" Matea whispered. She was still in pain, so she couldn't talk loudly.

"Yes, I am okay. Your daughters showed me the beach. I just wanted to see how you are doing, though. Do you need anything?" Sasha asked, holding Matea's hand.

"Yes, come closer," she said. Sasha leaned over to hear what she had to say. "If me don't get better, can you please help me daughter start a new life in the States with her sister? That is me only request."

Sasha could sense that Matea wouldn't be coming out of this illness, and even though Vanessa was a grown woman, she knew that she wouldn't be able to adapt right away to the fast pace of the States. Even Akiylah was still trying to cope with it. The vultures there would eat her alive because of her vulnerability to a new environment.

"Anything for you. Now get some rest," she commanded.

"Thank you so much," Matea said, falling asleep from the pills that were given to her when she first arrived.

She couldn't afford the medicine she needed in time, and now it was basically too late. Sasha even brought a nurse to take care of her. Matea didn't tell her daughters, but she only had about a month left to live. The cancer had spread throughout her body, causing a high percentage of her cells to shut down. The pain was so unbearable at times that she wanted to die right then and there.

Sasha pulled the blanket over her and dimmed the light once she was resting peacefully. She walked into the kitchen where the girls were making lunch.

"Ms. Sasha, me know that Momma is in bad condition. We don't have money to bury her when she dies. What will we do?" Vanessa asked. She was a year younger than Akiylah but was very attractive.

"When my son married your sister, all of you became a part of our family. We take care of family, so let me take care of that when we reach that point. Just let the nurse do her job. I would like to go to one of those festivals tonight," she said, smiling.

"Me will take you, but you will have to dress accordingly," Akiylah blurted out.

"So what am I going to wear?" Sasha replied.

"Come with me, and me will show you some of the stores we have around here. You look like you will be able to find something nice," Vanessa said excitedly.

* * *

Sasha, Vanessa, and Akiylah, walked into club Bada's, and the place was packed with men and women wearing next to nothing. Sasha was surprised that she was trying to hang out with the young crowd. She actually was fitting right in, wearing a scandalous one-piece dress that fit her curves to a T. Vanessa and Akiylah both had on colorful wrap-around dresses. Akiylah's ass was bigger than her sister's, but not by much. They all sat at the bar and ordered drinks.

"Thank you for bringing me out tonight, ladies. I think we all needed this right now," Sasha said over the loud Jamaican music playing.

"Are you having fun?" Vanessa asked.

"Yes!"

"Me miss me momma. Me want to go back home and make sure she alright," Akiylah said. She never liked going to parties. She only did it because she wanted to entertain Sasha.

"You can go back, and me will stay here with Ms. Sasha," Vanessa told her.

Akiylah gathered her belongings and rushed out of the club to get back home to her ill mother. If Vanessa would have known what the circumstances were, she would have left also.

"Dutty dutty dutty love love. I'm feeling like you letting go," Sasha's favorite song blasted through the speakers, causing her to move side to side in her seat. It must have been everyone else's favorite song as well, because the dance floor was packed. You could barely move anywhere. The women looked like they were ready to have sex right there. Sasha stood up and grabbed Vanessa's hand, pulling her out there with everyone else. The two started displaying their dance skills while the crowd formed a circle around them.

"Vanessa, I didn't know you could dance like that," Sasha stated, watching her go to the ground, then come back up. "Your movements are enticing."

"Me learned when me was six years old. All the girls use to have a dance challenge, and me would come in second or third place. Me only won one time," she said as they sat down to rest from all the dancing they had been doing.

As they talked, a couple of guys came over and sat next to them. One had very long dreads that came to his lower back. His accent piqued Sasha's interest when he asked her to dance. She told him that she was tired, but there was something about him that wouldn't take no for an answer. She decided to give him one dance, so they walked out to the floor. As if on cue, Beyoncé's and Usher's voices serenaded from the speakers:

Now baby girl there ain't nothing more that I can say. You know by now I want it more than anything. If I walk away now would you leave, you'll be stuck in my head like a melody. I know you want it, I'm hesitating (why?), you must be crazy, I got a man, you got a lady (I know). We here together, so this must be something special, you could be anywhere you wanted but you decided to be here with me. No coincidence, this was meant to be . . .

Sasha loved this song, and she let it be known by the way her body moved in his arms. He was enjoying the way her body felt grinding up against him, and his hardness was the proof of it. Sasha felt it too but was too caught up in the moment to have any control of the reaction that it was causing. She felt a tingle in her panties, causing her to press tighter than normal. The man with the dreads cupped her buttocks, grinding harder on her pelvis.

The music kept playing:

In this club, in this club, ladies when I put this love up on you one time if you ain't scared then say what's up. In this club, in this club, they can keep watching. I ain't stopping, baby, I don't give up . . .

"Let's take a walk to my office in the back," he whispered in her ear.

Sasha's eyes were closed until she heard that. They popped open, trying to adjust to the lights. She looked at the sexy man standing in front of her and smiled. "What for?"

"To get away from this noise and have some alone time. See, mon, me feeling you," he said, squeezing her ass.

She thought about it for a moment, and as tempted as she was, she couldn't just leave her daughter-in-law alone. Plus she didn't want either of them to get the wrong impression, even though she would have loved to jump his boner right now.

"I don't think that would be a good idea. I'm a married woman," she said, moving away from his grasp.

"Is he here with you?"

"No, he's home with my son."

"Well what he don't know, won't hurt him," he said, invading her personal space. "Me thought you came here to enjoy yourself. Me know you'll enjoy it."

"I came here with my daughter-in-law. You are very forward, but I just wanted to dance, not have sex in your or nobody else's office," she lied, feeling her juices running down her legs. He took the hint and walked away.

Sasha walked back over to where Vanessa and the other guy were. They were just about to leave. Vanessa saw her coming and met her halfway.

"Me about to go with him. Will you be okay? You know how to get back to the house, right?" she asked cheerfully.

Sasha noticed that she was tipsy and anxious to go with the young stud. Not trying to interfere with what they were about to do, she said okay. The two of them left, and Sasha had a couple more drinks before deciding to go home. The weather was nice, so she sat down in the sand on the beach, outside of Akiylah's mom's house.

"Would you like to take a stroll since you're here?" someone said, making Sasha turn around to the sound of his voice.

"Are you following me?" she asked playfully.

"No, me live right there," he said, pointing to the loft next to Matea's.

"I didn't know you were staying there. Well sure, let's go," she told him.

They walked along the sand just enjoying the breeze. Sasha held her sandals in one hand while holding onto his arm with the other. She had to admit to herself that she was feeling him. She wanted to try to salvage her marriage when she got home, but her addiction to sex was ruining that theory. The water washed over her toes, and his touch made her pussy throb. She wanted to sex him in the worst way, but she didn't want to seem easy, especially since she told him she had a husband and son at home.

She looked around to see if they were out there alone, but she already knew they were. Pressing his body against hers, the man with the dreads kissed her gently. Sasha could taste the salt from the misty air on his lips as he slipped his tongue into her mouth. Sasha gave in, pulling his shirttail from his pants, unbuttoning it and taking it off, then tossing it to the ground. She kissed his neck and chest, sucking his nipples and nipping at them with her teeth. He moaned his appreciation, but then she stopped and untied her wrap-around dress, showing off her supermodel body.

His eyes were stuck on her flat belly and hard thighs. She was wearing a skimpy black G-string that made her tan lines visible. He could see her lips trying to escape the thin fabric. With her dress flattened out on the sand, Sasha lay her half-naked body on top of it, motioning for him to join her. In one motion, he pulled off his shorts and boxers, then dropped to his knees, burying his face all over her body. He explored every part, starting from her neck and working his way down. He kissed the curve of her breasts and played with her erect nipples between his fingers.

Sticking one into his mouth, he began sucking on it, causing Sasha to let out a soft moan. She grabbed his dick and rubbed it against her thigh, trying to shift her hips in a way to align it with her pussy. Reaching between her legs, he ran his fingers along her slit. She was so wet that he easily slid two fingers inside her love tunnel.

"Oh shit, right there," Sasha screamed out in pleasure, moving her hips, forcing his fingers deeper inside.

She quickly followed his lead by reaching down and gripping his hard penis. As she slowly worked his cock, she felt an orgasm building up from his fingers pumping her vagina like a dick. She started grinding her hips against his fingers, and he gave her what she wanted, knowing that she was about to cum. Sasha pumped his dick faster, trying to make him cum also. The man grunted, trying to hold back, and rolled his thumb over her clit. Sasha began to shake uncontrollably, and she came hard over his finger. It was so powerful that she released his dick, then wrapped her arms around his neck tightly.

After her breathing slowed up, she took his dick and lined it up with her opening. He got the hint, thrusting his hips forward, pumping in and out of her wetness. Sasha wrapped her legs around his back and met him thrust for thrust.

"This is just what I needed right now," Sasha moaned, rocking back and forth.

"You are so wet. Me dick is soaked," he said, squeezing her ass cheeks together, making her body come up to meet his.

They were locked together on the beach, the ocean lapping at the shore behind them. A couple minutes later, Sasha flipped him over and began riding his dick like a cowgirl. He reached up and cupped her breasts in his hands, pinching her nipples lightly with the tip of his fingers. That made her even more turned on. She moved faster, slamming herself down against his pelvis on every stroke.

"Oh fuck, that feels good!" Sasha exclaimed, feeling another orgasm forming.

"Cum for me," he said, pumping harder.

"Here . . . it . . ." She never finished; she just erupted in an ear-piercing wail of relief as her pussy literally exploded. The onrush of her liquid orgasm suddenly leaped from within the soft pink folds of her pussy, bathing his dick in copious amounts of pearly thick cum cream. Like a woman that was possessed, she dug her nails into his back. He also was ready to cum from her warm insides as she continued to convulse on his shaft. His balls tightened up, and he pulled out just in time to shoot his load all over her pubic hairs.

After a little rest, they got up and attempted to brush the sand off of their bodies and clothes. It was still stuck to their skin, but they were so tired that they didn't care. She went home, and as soon as she fell on her bed, she went to sleep with a smile on her face. She had to see him one more time before she went back, because his sex game was on point.

* * *

Sahmeer and Marcus were spending some long overdue father-and-son time while Sasha and Akiylah were in the Virgin Islands. It seemed as if everything was starting to get back to normal, and Marcus couldn't have been happier. They were in the Sixers' practice facility playing a game of one-on-one basketball. Sahmeer was using that as a form of therapy for his leg. It was almost back at

100 percent, but he needed a few more sessions to make sure.

"Dad, you're getting beat by a man with one leg. You're losing your swagger," Sahmeer said jokingly.

"You're only up two points, and that's only because I'm letting you."

"Come on, old man, you know I'm better than you now. Remember, I have your genes inside me, so it's only right that I inherit your skills," he said, punching his dad in the arm.

That statement made him think about the secret they had been keeping from Sahmeer. He was tired of keeping it from him.

"Son, come here. I have something to tell you," Marcus said, sitting down on the bench. He was willing to accept whatever Sahmeer's reaction would be, as long as he knew the truth.

"What's up, Pop?" Sahmeer asked, wiping his face with one of the towels.

"I think you deserve to know that Kevin is . . ." he started to say, when his coach came out of the office.

"Marcus, I need to speak with you for a minute," the coach said, standing by the door.

"Go ahead, Dad. I'm going to shoot around for a few more minutes, then take a quick shower so I can go meet Mike. I'll see you when you get home."

"Okay, but we'll finish our conversation tonight. Do you need anything?"

"No, I'm good. Just sharpen up on your jump shot so next time you'll be able to present a challenge," he smirked, taking a shot. The ball hit nothing but net.

Marcus laughed at his son's joke because he knew Sahmeer couldn't beat him for real. Marcus was just trying to take it easy on him until he was at full capability. When he walked into his coach's office, he found out that Embiib would be taking Kevin's place in the starting lineup. His shooting and rebounding skills would be a much-needed improvement because of his youthfulness. He had just come back from an injury, so they would limit his minutes.

"Well, I'll see you tomorrow," Marcus stated, leaving the office.

When he got inside his car, he gave Morgan a call to see where he was. He had returned to Philly for a meeting with the mayor. They were about to appoint the new deputy commissioner, and it was going to be a big ceremony in city hall.

"What's up, superstar? How have you been?" Morgan said.

"I'm good, Morgan. I seen on the news that you were going to be here today, and was wondering if you wanted to hang out with me and Kevin tonight. He's been traded to Golden State, so we're going to give him a going away party," Marcus said, turning onto the expressway.

"Count me in! I haven't seen you guys in a while. Where are we going to meet, so I can give my security detail a heads-up?" Morgan said.

"You can meet us at the Hilton hotel, near the airport at around nine o'clock. We have the penthouse on the top floor all weekend."

"Okay, I'll see you later, Marcus," Morgan said, ending the call. Because of his political ties, he had to be discrete about what kind of fun he had and with who.

Marcus headed over to see an old friend before going home. He hasn't seen her in over two years and thought that it would be a nice surprise. When he pulled up to South Philly High School, better known as "Southern," everyone stared at his car trying to see who was getting out. When Marcus stepped out, the group of students knew exactly who he was. He stopped and gave out a few autographs before heading inside to talk to his friend. Security was tight at the door, but because of his celebrity status, he was easily let through.

"You can head up now, sir. She is in the classroom on the second floor at the end of the hall," one of the security staff told him.

When he approached the room, she had her back to him, so she didn't see him sneak up behind her. She was writing something on the board.

"Guess who?" he said, putting his hands over her eyes.

"Let me go before you get something you didn't ask for," she replied, grabbing his arms, trying to remove them from her face.

"I see you haven't changed," he said, releasing his grip. "What's up, Sis?"

She turned around and smiled when she saw her brother. She gave him a hug and then punched him in the arm.

"Where have you been? I haven't I heard from you in two years," she said.

"I'm sorry that I haven't spoken to you since the last time we spent Thanksgiving together. Your husband is the reason why that happened."

"We are family, Marcus. No one should ever come between us. I tried calling you, but you changed your number. I missed my brother and nephew. How are Sahmeer and Sasha doing?" she said, sitting at her desk.

Pamela was Marcus's lil sister. They had a fallout over her husband a couple years ago because he was drunk and crashed his car into Marcus's Benz. He didn't have insurance, so Marcus's insurance company ended up having to pay for the damages. He told him he would give him the money back but never did. Pamela thought it was petty, because Marcus was a rich NBA player and had more money than the both of them put together. To Marcus, it was the principle. He never thought that his own flesh and blood would put anyone before him. They were so close when they were kids, and that all changed when he went away to college and she enrolled in the army. He thought it was time to mend their relationship. That's why he was here.

"They both are doing okay. Sahmeer misses his auntie. He asks about you all the time."

"I know. We have dinner together once a month," she stated, surprising her brother. He didn't know that his son had kept in touch with her all this time.

"I was wondering if you would like to join us tonight to celebrate Kevin's going away party. He would love to see you before he leaves for Cali."

Pam hadn't seen Kevin since the last birthday party they had. The two of them almost had an affair but didn't go through with it. She loved her husband too much to deceive him like that.

"He's been traded?" she questioned.

"Yes, to Golden State."

"Wow, that's good for him. Sure, I'll go to the party, as long as I have my brother back in my life?"

"I wouldn't be here if you didn't," he replied, giving Pam a kiss on the cheek. "I will see you at the party then. I will text you with the address."

"Okay, should I bring anything?"

"No, just dress to impress like you always do. Love you," he said, walking toward the door.

"Love you too," she said as her students started piling into the room.

She was glad that she finally saw her brother. She always watched his games on television, but never had the courage to call. She wasn't telling her husband about the party. This would be one that she went to alone.

NINE

RAPHAEL AND CARLA WERE helping Elaina get settled in with Christopher. They all redecorated the guest room so they would be comfortable. Raphael didn't know how long they would be there, but he hoped it wouldn't be long. Carla was sitting on the couch watching *The Steve Harvey Show*, when Elaina came down the steps with Christopher in hand.

"We have to go out for a while, but we'll be back in a couple of hours," she said, heading for the door.

"I'm making dinner for us if you want some," Carla said.

"That's fine, thank you," Elaina said, shutting the door behind her.

Carla waited for the show to go off, then headed into the kitchen to start dinner. Raphael walked in as she was bending over the stove, and grabbed her waist.

"Did you miss me?" she asked, already knowing the answer.

"Does this answer your question?" he replied, poking her ass with his erect penis.

"Definitely," she said, moving her ass around on his shaft.

"We have a few minutes. You trying to have some fun?" he asked seductively, already pulling her clothes off before she had a chance to reply.

"Really?" she said wickedly as he began struggling out of his own clothing. "What if Elaina comes back early?"

"Well, then, I guess she'll see something she doesn't want to," he replied.

It was funny what the mere thought of fucking Carla right then and there could do to him. They were both so horny at that point that they could care less who came through those doors. Standing behind her, he pulled her panties to the side, then buried his hard dick deep inside her tight wet hole.

Carla started moaning and groaning with so much pleasure each time he hit her spot. He loved hearing her tell him how good his dick felt inside of her walls. It was driving both of them crazy as he sped up his pace.

"Oh, baby! Baby! Yes, fuck me, fuck me! Just like that. Oh yes. Harder," she kept saying.

He was only too happy to oblige. Raphael was just getting into it when he happened to glance up momentarily and catch a glimpse of Elaina's face peering around the corner of the kitchen door. He almost said something but thought better of it when she disappeared from view. The fact that they were being watched boosted the pleasure tenfold and it gave Raphael a deliciously wicked little chuckle. He could only imagine what she must be thinking.

After a few more minutes of mind-blowing sex, Carla stopped because she wanted to taste his dick in her mouth. She loved doing it to him more than she did her ex-husband. Raphael stood there as she got down between his legs, working his cock slowly over her tongue before trying to swallow it.

Raphael glanced up, catching movement once again in the area he had seen Elaina a few minutes ago. He realized that she had no clue that he could see her standing there. She tried to get a better look by presenting herself more clearly to enjoy the show. Raphael was now finding this weird little scene quite erotic. Having an audience was a bit kinky to him and was one of his fantasies. They both began moaning and groaning loudly, in unison with each other. Carla became so hot that she started fingering herself while still busily sucking on his dick.

To Raphael's surprise, he watched Carla slip her hand inside the sweatpants she was wearing and inside her panties, stroking her pussy. She watched as Carla continued giving him a dominant blow job.

"Oh fuck, Carla!" he shouted. "You're gonna make me cum if you keep doing that."

She was on the verge of an orgasm herself through the use of her own fingers. Each stroke was bringing her closer and closer to reaching that ultimate high.

"Cum for me, baby. Let it all out!" she urged just as loudly. "Fucking cum for me. Shoot that hot white cream into my mouth, baby."

There was no doubt that he was seconds away from doing just that too! Especially glancing up to see Elaina's hand furiously working itself beneath her panties, the other caressing a single breast which she'd exposed by lifting up a portion of her shirt. That was more than he could handle. A combination of seeing Elaina touching herself and Carla's incredible mouth working it's magic, soon had him over the edge.

He felt the first hot load of his sperm filling Carla's mouth, his eyes suddenly closing shut, and the sound of his own voice suddenly filling the air. "Oh fuck, baby! Fuck! Fuck that feels good."

Carla took it all in like a pro. She wiped the semen over her body, then licked her fingers. Raphael looked over in the direction of Elaina, and she was gone. They both fixed their clothing and went upstairs to their room.

* * *

The party was in full swing by time Kevin and Marcus had arrived. There were so many people there that half of them were partying in the pool. Kevin knew that Marcus was throwing him a going away party, but never had he imagined it being like this.

"You really know how to throw a man a party," Kevin stated, looking at all the half-naked women lurking around everywhere.

"I just wanted you to see what you'll be leaving behind. We will all miss you, bro."

"You'll get to see me. It ain't like we're not going to hang out anymore. Just 'cause I'll be all the way across the map, it doesn't mean that I won't come back to visit. Plus, I'm going to beat you when we play your team," he joked.

"In your dreams, bro, in your dreams," Marcus said, patting him on the back.

They grabbed a glass of champagne from the lady walking around in a G-string, then proceeded out to the balcony. Marcus's eyes lit up when he saw Pam standing out there looking so beautiful.

"Is that your sister right there?" he asked, already knowing the answer. He just couldn't believe that she was here. To him, she was always the girl that got away.

"Yeah, that's her! Why don't you go over there and say hi. I'll be mingling with a few of our friends to see who wants to bet on the game," Marcus said, walking off.

Kevin eased past a couple of people, making his way over to Pam and one of her friends. She turned around just as he was approaching.

"Well who do we have here?" he asked.

"Kevin, how have you been?" she said, giving him a hug. The two embraced for a couple of minutes before releasing their grasp. "Sorry about what happened to Michelle."

"Thank you! I've been good, just taking it easy! I know you already heard from your brother that I'm leaving for Cali?"

"That shit is all over ESPN. How could I not see that? Just don't forget about us like you did before," she said, trying to make him feel guilty.

"Pam, we were so young back then. Besides, your brother was like my brother. Sometimes I do wish that I would have asked to be your man. Maybe we would still be together now. Who knows?" he replied.

"Do you remember what you said our song would have been if we would have gone to the prom together?"

"How could I forget? I use to sing it every time I heard it," Kevin said, blushing. She was probably the only one that made him feel like putty. "Wait a second, I'll be right back."

Kevin walked over to where the DJ had set up his equipment, and whispered something to him. The DJ nodded his head and shook Kevin's hand. Kevin walked back over to where Pamela and her friends were standing, smiling at her.

"Would you like to dance with me just for one song?"

"Kevin, I know you didn't do what I think you did," she said, giving him a crazy look.

"Well because of my previous engagement, we never had the chance to have that dance. So I thought that since this was my last week here, why not get my dance from a beautiful lady?"

"Well since you put it that way." Pam sat her drink down on one of the coasters on the table. She grabbed him by the hand as he led her to the floor.

He signaled to the DJ, who hit a button on his equipment that changed the music. Pam smiled as soon as she heard the intro.

"I see you didn't forget the song," she said, placing her arms around his neck.

Keith Sweat sang out over the speakers:

I wanna tease you, I wanna please you, I wanna show baby, that I need you. I want your body, til the very last drop, I want you to holler, til you want me to stop. And who can love you like me, nobody, who can treat you like me, nobody, and who can lay your body down, nobody baby . . .

The song had everyone grinding on each other.

"I will never forget this song, Pam. Even when Michelle was alive and I heard this song, I thought about you."

"You're just saying that to make me feel good," she said, smiling at him.

"I'm serious! This will always be our song," he told her. They held each other tightly until the song ended. Then Trey Songz blazed the speakers: "We were so dumb in love, couldn't get enough no, but I could have loved you so much better, and I can't believe you never walked out, and it's not your fault, that I fumbled your heart . . ."

"I love this song," Pam said, grabbing him again. "I think he wrote this just for me."

"Sure he did."

They both laughed as they enjoyed the music: *"Should have let go of my past for you. You did everything I asked of you. Travel cross the country if I asked you to, but I'm just bad for you. I fumbled your heart . . ."*

They danced to a couple more songs before the music stopped and everyone gathered around for a toast. Marcus toasted to their many years of friendship and hoped that it never ended. It was getting late, so Pam was ready to leave. She gave her brother a hug goodbye then walked over to where Kevin was standing.

"If I don't get the chance to see you before you leave, good luck," she said, giving him a hug. Kevin kissed her softly on the lips, and she hesitated before pulling back. "Kevin, we can't do this. I'm engaged to be married."

"What?"

"I said I'm getting married," she repeated.

"Why didn't you tell me this?" he said, finally noticing the big-ass rock on her finger. He was a little tipsy from all the liquor he had earlier. "I don't care about him."

Kevin grabbed Pam by the waist and tried to kiss her again. This time she put her hand on his chest, pushing him away. He was persistent on getting his kiss, gripping her arm tighter.

"Kevin, let me go. You're drunk," she said, trying to pull away.

Marcus heard the commotion when the DJ stopped the music, and looked in that direction to see who it was. When he saw that it was his sister and friend, he rushed over there. He pushed Kevin back, away from Pam.

"What are you doing to my sister, man?"

"She led me on tonight, making me think that we were going to be together. Now she talking about she's engaged," Kevin said, slurring his words.

"You're drunk, man. I think it's time to take you home," Marcus said, trying to help his friend walk away.

Kevin yanked away from him, walking back toward Pam. "Come here, baby. I just want to sample the goods before I never see you again." He grabbed Pam's ass and squeezed it.

"I said let's go," Marcus said firmly, this time a little too loudly.

By this time, they had drawn a crowd as people gathered around to see what the commotion was. Sahmeer and Mike heard the noise and walked over to where they were. Marcus tried to forcefully help Kevin out the door, but Kevin was persistent about getting in Pam's panties.

"What, you want me to pay you for some pussy?" he said, pulling out a wad of cash, then throwing it at her. "You're just like all these other money-hungry bitches."

"You're out of line, Kevin. Let's go," Marcus once again said, trying to push his friend out the door.

"Get the fuck off of me. Fuck that bitch!" Kevin yelled, then smacked the hell out of Pam. She fell to the floor, holding her face.

"What the fuck . . . ?" Marcus snapped, punching him dead in the jaw.

Mike and Sahmeer ran over and helped Kevin up as a couple other people pulled Marcus back. He tried to get at him again but couldn't.

"Don't you ever put your hands on my sister again," Marcus said, pulling away from the two men holding him, and fixing his clothes. "Come on, Sahmeer, we are leaving!"

"My son can stay here if he wants to," Kevin said. Marcus gave Kevin a look of death. "Oh, so you didn't tell him yet, huh?"

Sahmeer looked puzzled because he thought he was talking about Mike. Kevin had a smirk on his face as if he had just won the lottery. Everyone was staring, waiting to see what was about to happen next.

"Mike, take your dad home," Marcus told Mike.

"Tell your son what I'm talking about," Kevin said, wiping the blood from his mouth. "Or should I tell him?"

"Dad, what's going on? What is he talking about?" Sahmeer asked, looking at his father for answers.

"Nothing! Mike, get him out of here."

"Dad, come on, let's go home," Mike said, trying to take his father home.

"I'll leave when I get ready to. Sahmeer, I'm your father! Me and Sasha had an affair when we were younger, and she ended up pregnant. That's why he couldn't give you the transfusion you needed, because he wasn't a match."

There was a loud gasp as people tried to take in what they just heard. The place was so silent that you could hear a pin drop. Sahmeer couldn't believe what he was hearing. This was the second time his father had deceived him, and this was the last straw.

"I have to get the fuck out of here," Sahmeer snapped, running out the door.

He got on the elevator and took it all the way down to the lobby. When he got off, he noticed that the bar was still open, so he went inside. For the next hour, he ordered drink after drink, until the bartender wouldn't serve him anymore.

"Sir, are you staying here at the hotel?" she asked.

"Why?"

"Because I cannot let you drive home like that. I have a room here if you would like to rest until you sober up," she stated.

"You don't know what the fuck I've been through tonight," he said, downing the rest of his drink.

"So why don't you tell me all about it," she said, giving him her undivided attention. "By the way, my name is Tiara!"

"I'm Sahmeer," he replied, trying to get up but losing his balance.

She came from behind the counter to help him up. He couldn't walk, so she helped him sit down in the chair.

"Your dad is that basketball player, right? I see y'all on TV together all the time with your mom, and I guess that other girl is your wife?" she said, sitting across from him.

"I need another drink, and I need to get the hell out of here. Do your job and go get my drink, whoever you are," Sahmeer demanded.

Tiara didn't budge. Instead she placed her hand on his leg. She moved it closer and closer toward his penis, with the hopes of seducing him. He jumped when she grabbed it.

"You need to calm down and let me take care of you. There are so many ways I can do it, if you let me," she whispered in his ear, massaging his semi-erect penis.

"I'm married, bitch, and stop trying to take advantage of me. I'm getting out of here. I'll take an Uber home," he said, regaining his composure, then standing up. He threw a hundred-dollar bill on the counter and walked out.

Tiara watched him leave, then walked over to where a customer had been sitting and watching the whole thing. She placed a drink on the table, looked around to make sure no one was paying them any attention, then passed the envelope back.

"He wouldn't do it!"

"I know. I seen the whole thing. Keep the money. You've earned it. Thank you for doing that. I know it felt like you were degrading yourself."

"Just let me know if you need me again," she said, getting up and leaving before someone saw them together.

The person she was talking to waited a few more minutes before exiting the bar and heading for the hotel's garage. "I'll get you sooner or later!"

TEN

BY SOME MIRACLE, THE medicine that Sasha's nurse brought for Matea not only cured her but altogether destroyed the virus that was running through her body. Everyone thought she would die because of how it ate at her cells, but that wouldn't be the case, at least for now. She lay in her bed sleeping peacefully from the antibiotics that were injected into her.

"Thank you so much for saving our mother," Vanessa said to the nurse, giving her a hug. "You didn't have to come all the way out here, but you did."

"I just came to see the water and take a vacation," she grinned, causing everyone to smile. "Well you got a chance to do both, and we still have other things to do if you like? Me can take you on a boat ride," Akiylah stated, chiming in.

The ringing of Sasha's cell phone interrupted their girly session. She answered it while the girls sat at Matea's bedside.

"Shit just hit the fan. You need to come home now," the caller said.

"What happened?"

"Kevin and Marcus had a fight at the party last night, and Kevin told Sahmeer that he was his father. It must have been true, because Marcus didn't even try to defend it. Is it true, Sasha?"

"I am catching the next flight back today," she said, not even responding to the question. She hit the end button and looked up at Akiylah.

"You okay?" Akiylah asked, sensing that something was wrong.

"Yes, I have to go home!" she said, heading into the other room to pack.

There were a million questions running through her mind, and she had to get home to get them answered. She tried calling her son's phone, but it went straight to voicemail. When she called Marcus to find out what was going on, his also went to voicemail. As a last resort, she called Kevin, and he answered on the first ring.

"Kevin, what happened last night?"

"He needed to know, and I don't regret telling him."

"I asked you to wait until the time was right, but you just had to open your mouth. A drunk mind really speaks a sober tongue! Why were you two fighting anyway?" Sasha asked, closing her bag.

"Because he is mad that the Warriors chose me over him, and he tried to disrespect me in front of everybody," Kevin lied.

"Have you heard from my son? He's not answering his phone, and I'm getting worried!"

"Not since he stormed out of there. He did it at my god damn going away party, Sasha. What was I supposed to do, let him humiliate me just like that?"

She could hear him slurring his words as he talked, so she assumed he was still drunk from the night before. At this point she didn't give a damn, because her son was her priority. What was he going to think of her now?

"No, you could have kept your mouth shut about that, but it's too late, so now I have to once again do damage control and figure out where to go from here."

"Sorry, Sasha, it just came out," he said, starting to feel a bit guilty about the situation.

"You're not sorry, Kevin. You're careless and reckless, that's all. I'm on my way home. I have to find my son and make sure he is okay. If you see him or my husband, tell them to call me immediately," she said, ending the call before he had a chance to reply.

In the next two hours, Sasha had made it to the airport and was in the air on her way home. Akiylah and Vanessa came along for support, leaving the nurse there with their mother.

* * *

Sahmeer woke up the next morning with a splitting headache. He was lying in the backseat of his Range Rover. He didn't remember anything that happened the night before after the bar, not even how he ended up where he was. When he looked around, he noticed that he was still in the parking lot at the hotel.

"Damn, I must have drank too much liquor last night," he said to himself, removing his iPhone from his pocket.

Once he saw his mom's and dad's numbers, everything came back and hit him like a ton of bricks. His hatred for his dad turned toward his mother also. His whole life consisted of one great big lie! Instead of calling any of them back, he headed home to take a shower and grab some clothes.

Pulling into the driveway was like pulling up to an illusion of what his life used to be. Sahmeer hoped that no one would be there so that he could get in and out. To his surprise, his physical therapist was there. She was doing yoga, and Sahmeer couldn't help but notice that she was wearing tights with no panties. It wasn't a surprise to see her there. After all, she had a key to the house. He thought he was done with therapy.

"Hey," he said, startling her.

"Sahmeer, I didn't know you were coming back home so soon. I hope you don't mind me being here."

"No, I don't mind at all. I really had a tough evening, and it's not going to get any easier," he stated, sitting down on the couch.

"You wanna talk about it? I'm a very good listener!" She smiled.

Sahmeer really needed someone to vent to, and since she had been around the family so long, he decided to take her up on that offer. He motioned for her to sit down, and once she did, he dropped the bombshell on her. Lorena couldn't believe what he told her, but at the same time she understood his parents' reasons for not saying anything.

"I just wish they would have told me, instead of me finding out like that. Maybe I would have handled it differently."

"Your parents love you very much, Sahmeer. They have provided you with everything you could ever want. You have to give them at least the chance to explain their side."

"What if they lie about it?" he asked her.

"It's always three sides to a story, but it will be up to you to decide which is the truth. Follow your heart," she replied, placing her hand over his. They both felt the spark shoot through their bodies, and then they kissed.

Neither one of them were expecting that to happen, it just did. Sahmeer had so much pain built up inside that Lorena's words were so soothing to him. His hand made its way to one of her breasts and squeezed it gently.

"You sure you want to do this? I don't want you to do something that you'll regret!" she moaned, getting turned on from his touch.

He never responded, pinching her nipple through the shirt she was wearing. She let out a soft moan, rubbing his manhood through the khakis he had on. She removed her shirt to give him better access to her swollen nipples.

"Oh my, is this really happening?" she said as his hand slowly moved up her thigh.

He kissed her neck and shoulders while his hand massaged her pussy. He felt the heat coming from her body, her juices leaking through the tights indicating her wetness. Lorena let out a gasp and almost came on herself. His kisses continued to travel up to her breasts, and he gave them a sensual kiss. Impulsively, she put her hands under her breasts and held them up to him. Passion quickly overtook them, and he pulled her tights off, then removed his clothes.

"This is what I need right now," he told her, lying down on the yoga mat.

She stroked his erection, noticing that he was endowed with a huge penis. She wanted to feel it inside her ASAP.

"Let me get a condom to put on," he said, reaching into his pocket.

Glad that he had one, she took it and slipped it over the head, then rolled it all the way down its length to his balls. He kept teasing her with the head, rubbing it over her clitoris, then sticking it in a little, then pulling it back out.

"Please, I want you to fuck me now!"

"If you really insist," he replied, pushing all the way into her throbbing moist cunt.

The joy of his dick inside her caused her to moan with pleasure as she came over and over again. Sahmeer followed with a breathtaking eruption of his own. When she regained her senses, she took Sahmeer's softening penis into her mouth and in no time had it fully erect again. She couldn't get enough of it and whimpered with lust as she struggled to deep throat his entire shaft.

"Damn, you can suck a dick," he said, trying to compliment her on her skills.

She was ready to gulp down his creamy sperm, when he suddenly pulled away from her, his dick popping out of her mouth like a cork.

"What's wrong?" she wondered, thinking something was wrong.

"I have something special for you, baby. Turn around!"

Lorena got on all fours, and Sahmeer got behind her, coated his dick with lubricant, and prepared to penetrate her asshole. She trembled in happy anticipation, realizing that his dick was about to be stuffed into her virgin hole. Carefully he eased his penis into her, her asshole stretching widely to accommodate his thick girth.

"Ouuuchhh," she screamed out in pleasure and pain. This was something new to her, and she didn't know why she was letting him do it.

Once he was fully inside, he began a slow, steady stroke, building up to a comfortable rhythm that soon had her pleading for more. Lorena was loving the feeling of anal sex so much that she reached down and started fingering her clit. She came twice before Sahmeer pulled his dick out of her quivering ass and squirted his load all over her cheeks.

"I see why you're a good therapist," Sahmeer said, putting his clothes back on. "You bring out the best in your clients."

"You wasn't so bad yourself," she replied, wiping herself with the towel she had left on the floor.

Before Sahmeer pulled his pants all the way up, Lorena also wiped his dick off. She put her clothes back on, then cleaned up the mess they just made. Sahmeer didn't say anything, he just headed up to his room. He didn't feel any guilt about what he had done. He just wished that the pain and deception he was feeling would go away.

"If you need anything, let me know," he hollered down to Lorena.

"I think you gave me enough," she stated under her breath as she headed out the door. She didn't even tell him she was leaving.

* * *

Mike was standing over his dad as he slept peacefully, trying to recover from all the liquor he had the night before. He held a Glock 9 mm in his hand and was twisting a silencer on it. The sinister look in his eyes had danger written all over it.

"Dad, I'm sorry about this! Everybody is ruining everything right now, but I will fix it," he stated, cocking one in the chamber.

Tears welled up in his eyes as he realized what he was about to do. The only time he had ever fired his weapon was at the gun range. That was nothing compared to what he was planning to do. He peaked out the window, making sure no one else was outside. He aimed his gun, index finger gently pressing on the trigger. Just before the gun went off, he heard an SUV pulling into the driveway.

Mike quickly put the safety back on and tucked his gun inside his waist. When he looked out to see who had pulled up, he saw Sasha, Akiylah, and another beautiful girl exiting the car. The Uber driver grabbed their bags from the trunk and placed them in front of the door.

"Do you need any help?" Mike asked, walking over toward them.

"No thank you, we have it," Sasha replied, stopping him in his tracks.

He could tell that she wasn't in a very good mood, and backed off. The look on her face told him everything he needed to know. Shit was about to hit the fan! A secret that she had kept in the dark all this time had finally come to light. Akiylah gave him a smile but didn't say anything. Vanessa also glanced over in his direction as they headed inside the house.

"Come out back in ten minutes," he mouthed to her when she looked at him again. She nodded in agreement, then closed the door behind them. Mike ran upstairs to put the gun away, before heading out back.

It didn't take her long to sneak out and meet him at their usual spot in the guest house. Mike was already inside when she walked in. He pinned her up against the wall, holding her arms so she couldn't move. The thought of being handled aggressively made her pussy wet, and ready for something long and hard to fill it up. This wasn't no booty call, though, and she could tell by the way he gripped her throat.

"Are you ready to prove your love for me?" he said, gritting his teeth. She couldn't speak, so she nodded her head. "I need you to do something for me, and then I'll show you my gratitude."

He ripped her shirt open, then unzipped her jeans and stuck a finger into her pussy. She tried to reach for his penis but couldn't. He stuck two more fingers inside her pussy, making sure he paid special attention to her clit.

"Mmmmmm," she moaned closing her eyes and leaning her head back against the wall.

"Tell me that you want me," he whispered in her ear.

"Please fuck me and stop teasing me!"

Mike felt her about to cum and pulled his fingers out. She opened her eyes when she felt him zipping up her jeans. He backed away from her, removing his shirt and passing it to her. She took it and slipped it on. Her pussy was dripping all through her panties. She got on her hands and knees then crawled toward him.

"Get your ass up off that floor! It's time to show me how far you're willing to go," he replied, helping her get up.

"Anything you want," she said, giving him her full attention.

He disappeared upstairs for a couple of minutes, returning with his gun in hand. She got nervous when he sat it down on the table next to her. He sensed that nervousness but didn't care. All he cared about was the task at hand.

"Now this is what I need you to do, so pay attention . . ."

ELEVEN

"I REALLY APPRECIATE YOU letting us stay here with you and Raphael. We won't be here too long, I promise," Elaina said as she and Carla sat at the table drinking coffee.

"That's not a problem. Stay as long as you need," Carla replied.

"It's nice to see Ralph happy again. I really think he deserves it, especially since the way it ended between us."

"I'll never let that happen between us, and since we're on the subject, why did y'all split up?" Carla asked.

"We both had different views on relationships! Basically he didn't want a monogamous relationship and I did. That's why I tip my hat to you for breaking him out of that. It shows that he must love you more than he loved me," Elaina said, staring at Carla.

She could see why he picked Carla: she was one of the most beautiful women Elaina had ever seen. Her body was flawless except for a few marks on her legs. All and all, she definitely could have graced the cover of any magazine.

"Thank you! Just don't try to steal my man back," Carla joked.

"He's all yours," she replied, thinking about when she watched them having sex.

Raphael walked into the kitchen with little Chris. Carla admired the way Raphael had taken him in and treated him like he was his even though the test didn't come back yet. He gave Carla a kiss, then poured himself a glass of orange juice.

"I'm going to take Chris with me to the center to play while I teach my piano lesson, if that's okay with you."

"Sure, have fun, lil man!" she said, giving Chris a kiss on the cheek. "I'll stay here and help Carla straighten up."

"Alright, we'll see you later then!"

The boys left out, and Carla and Elaina began cleaning the house. They turned on the surround sound, and Alicia Keys came through the speakers. They started from downstairs and worked their way up. Once they were finished, Elaina started redecorating her room to her liking.

Carla went into her room to get ready to take a shower. After all the cleaning they had done to the house, it was time to clean herself. She stripped down, leaving her clothes on the floor, then entered the bathroom. Looking at herself in the mirror, tears started falling from her eyes. She thought about everything that had happened to her in the last two years.

"How did I get myself into this situation?" she said out loud to the mirror as if it would talk back to her.

She opened up the cabinet doors and pulled out the pill bottles that were sitting inside. After taking the medicine, she turned on the hot water, then stepped inside. The water was very soothing to her body, and she was caught up in the moment as her hand made its way to her breast. She began pinching her nipple, wishing that it was Raphael's mouth. Her other hand had found her clitoris and was working it overtime.

"Ahhhhh shit," she moaned, feeling herself about to cum.

She pumped her finger over her clit harder as the orgasm built up inside her. Seconds later her juices were all over her fingers. She stuck them in her mouth, licking them like it was his dick she was sucking.

"Carla, do you want to go to the mall with me?" Elaina called out, causing Carla to end her daydream.

"Sure, I'll be done in a few minutes."

Elaina kept talking to her as she looked through her closet for something. When she found what she was looking for, a smile came across her face. "Found it!" she whispered.

"Did you say something?" Carla asked, walking into the bedroom startling her, wearing nothing but her robe.

"Nothing, I was just admiring your wardrobe. Carla, you have lovely taste," she said, closing the closet. "Let me know when you're ready! I'll be downstairs waiting for you."

"Help me pick something out to wear. If you see something you like, you can borrow it if you want."

"Thanks, but I'm just going to throw on something out of my closet." She smiled.

"Okay, suit yourself! Well I will be ready to go in about fifteen minutes," Carla said, dropping her robe to the floor then walking over to her dresser and pulling out a panty and bra set.

Elaina watched her bend over to put on her panties. She felt the heat rising from her own panties and left the room before she acted on impulse. She headed downstairs, taking a deep breath. She wondered if she tried her if she would resist or go with the flow.

"Get it together, girl. You're strickly dickly," she said with a smile on her face and lust in her heart.

* * *

Ring, ring, ring! The sound of the doorbell interrupted Kevin's workout. He tried to ignore it because he didn't feel like being bothered, but it went off once again. *Ring, ring, ring!*

"Damn it! Who is it?" he yelled, walking toward the door.

He looked through the window, pausing momentarily before unlocking the door. He stood there wondering what she wanted.

"If you're here to say something about what happened last night, then go back home. He deserved to know what was going on."

"This is for you! Hope it makes you feel better," she said, stepping inside, closing the door behind her.

"What are you talking about?" he asked.

"Isn't this what you wanted?" she said, opening the wraparound dress she was wearing, and pulling it off.

Kevin stood there with his mouth wide open. She made sure that it stayed that way by dropping to her knees. In one quick motion, she had his penis out of his shorts and into her mouth. He fell against the wall as she deep throated him. He grabbed her head, pushing himself in and out of her wet mouth.

"Holy shit, that feels good," he moaned.

She used her hand and started fondling his balls while sucking furiously on his dick. It didn't take long for him to shoot his load down her throat. She stood up, wiping her mouth with the bottom of his shirt. She then put her dress back on and walked out of the house without saying a word.

"Where are you going? I need some pussy now!" he said, standing in the door with his limp penis still sticking out of his shorts.

She stopped, turned around, then blew him a kiss. "That's all for now. Enjoy your going-away present," she said, turning back around and heading in the house.

Kevin stepped back inside and shut the door. He opened the box to find a very expensive bottle of champagne inside. He removed it, popped the cork, and took a swig. It tasted good, so he drank some more of it as he sat down on the couch. Before he knew it, he had downed half the bottle. His eyes were blurry, and his head started spinning. He tried to get up and go upstairs but couldn't even make it to the steps before collapsing. He didn't know what was happening but knew it wasn't normal. The last thing he saw was the door opening back up, before everything around him went black.

"Is he, he dead?" she asked, looking at his body with her hand over her mouth.

"No, he's not dead yet, but if we don't get what we want, then . . ." he said, not finishing the statement. "Help me get him into the garage."

The two of them lifted Kevin's body and pulled him into the garage, where a black van was waiting.

They lifted him inside, closed the door, then went back inside.

"Come on, we have to make it look like a robbery slash kidnapping. Go upstairs and throw a few things around, then get back down here so we can leave. Don't take too long either. Now go!" he said, turning over tables and chairs.

They spent no less than ten minutes destroying anything and everything they could before getting up out of there. She didn't know it yet, but she was in way over her head. This could land her in Muncy State Correctional facility for a very long time if they get caught. She was too blinded by love to care, though.

"Time for the next phase of the plan," he said, driving off.

"What are you going to do now?"

"I already told you: the less you know, the better. I'm dropping you off at the next corner! You need to get back and be my eyes and ears, okay?"

She nodded her head yes and didn't say anything else. When she got out of the van, he jumped onto the expressway and headed to his destination. He wanted to hurry up and get back before shit hit the fan, because it sure as hell was about to.

* * *

Carla and Elaina returned from the mall at four o'clock in the afternoon to find Raphael over the stove cooking dinner. They stood at the door watching him dance to a Julio Iglesias song. He turned around when Chris looked up and saw his mother.

"Mommy!" he yelled, happy to see her.

When Raphael looked at them, they both were laughing. He smiled back and hunched his shoulders like he didn't know what they were laughing at.

"Don't mind us. Keep shaking that ass," Carla said, smiling. She pulled out some ones and held them in the air. "I have a tip for you if you drop it like it's hot."

That sparked a laugh from all of them, even lil Chris, and he didn't know what they were talking about. He just did it because everyone else was! Raphael told them all to take a seat while he made their plates. The food was fantastic, from the salad to the catfish. They talked about anything and everything they could think of. The way he admired Carla made Elaina feel just a bit of jealousy. She never could get him to feel that way about her.

"This was really good, Raphael! I'm going to put Chris to bed," Elaina said, noticing that he was sleepy.

"Let me do it, and y'all find a movie on Netflix," Raphael replied.

He carried Chris upstairs to his room. By the time Chris's head hit the pillow, he was out like a light. Raphael walked back down to the living room just as the movie was about to begin. He sat next to Carla on the couch, pressing the play button on the television.

"This is a really good movie right here," Carla said, referring to the movie called *Temptation*. It had a list of A-list celebrities in it.

They were in the middle of the movie at the part when he was eating her pussy on the plane, when Carla stuck her hand inside Raphael's sweatpants. She was trying to be spontaneous for a change, and from the look on his face, she could tell he was enjoying it. Elaina saw what she was doing but acted like she wasn't paying attention. Carla first started jerking him slowly. Then when she felt him tightening up, she quickened the pace. Sixty seconds later, he was shooting his load in his pants. They looked at each other and smiled knowing what had just happened.

Once the movie ended, Carla and Raphael retired to the confinements of their room, leaving Elaina downstairs still watching television. Once inside their room, clothes came off, and they made love until they both fell asleep.

Elaina watched a couple more movies before also falling asleep. When she woke up it was two thirty in the morning, and she realized that the TV had been watching her. She made a cup of hot chocolate, then sat in front of the fireplace. She heard someone coming down the steps, and when she looked up, it was Raphael.

"Couldn't sleep either?" Elaina asked him. He sat down next to her on the plush carpet floor.

"No! It's going to be a long day tomorrow at the center. We are hosting a sweet-sixteen party for one of the director's daughters."

"Sounds like it's going to be fun. If you need help, let me know. I won't be doing anything tomorrow anyway," she told him.

"That's generous of you! Maybe you can. Do you want to help with the food?"

"Anything I can do to help out! Well let me go get some rest," she replied standing up. She stood there looking down at him. "Thank you again for everything you're doing for us."

He looked up at the short robe she was wearing and stared at the silk panties she had on underneath.

"Oh yeah, I forgot to tell you that the test results will be back by the end of the week. I had them expedite the paperwork straight here, so FedEx will be dropping it off," he replied, trying to stand but falling back down.

He reached out for anything to stop the fall and grabbed Elaina, pulling her back down with him. She landed on top of him, and they laughed at each other. He tried to get up, but she was still on top of him. She took that as an opportunity and tried to kiss him. To her surprise, he kissed her back. It had been building up since he saw her watching him and Carla having sex.

"Mmmmm," she moaned, sucking on his bottom lip.

He turned her over, laying her on the rug, then opened her robe, exposing her caramel skin. He lifted up just enough to remove her panties. Raphael pulled away from her mouth and kissed each nipple, sucking them into his mouth gently but tightly. Just the sensation of his hands stroking her legs, and his tongue on her sensitive nipples, brought her to an orgasm.

Raphael entered her with two fingers, working them like a dick. She grabbed his wrist, guiding it into her wetness.

"Right there, baby. Just like that," she said.

She worked her hips in deep circles as his fingers thrashed in and out of her vagina. Raphael used two then three fingers, sliding them in, rubbing her wet clit, then pushing them back deep inside her. She felt something inside her pussy awakening, making it feel really good. His fingers were making a motion inside her as she arched her back and spread her legs wider, trying to stuff his whole arm inside. Before she knew it, something hot and delicious tore through her body and sent a gush of cum running out all over the rug.

As she came, he drove his hand deeper inside her pussy, hitting her G-spot, and she loved every minute of it. He removed a condom from its wrapper, wanting to fuck now, but she had other plans.

"Lay down on your back, baby," she whispered in his ear, trying not to wake Carla up.

She held his throbbing dick in her hand, amazed at how hard and thick it was. She slowly covered the head with her lips, then placed the whole thing into her mouth, working all the way down to his balls without gagging. Elaina licked and sucked him with so much love that his dick was glistening wet and twice as hard as when she started. He was pushing her head down hard and fast. She could feel his body tensing up and shivering with each lick.

"Not like that," he said, pulling her on top of him, holding her waist.

"What you gonna do?"

"Is this what you want," he said placing the condom on and guiding his dick into her hole.

"Yes, this is what I've been waiting for since I seen you and Carla together," she admitted, out of breath.

Elaina rode his dick like it was a bull, raising her ass up in the air, then slamming her body back down on his shaft. She did that over and over, pausing to rock and whimper every so often, until neither one could take it anymore.

"I'm cumming," she moaned, moving faster.

"Me too," he said, holding her waist as they came together.

He stood up and thought about what he had just done. It was too late to feel guilty now; the damage was done, and they both enjoyed it. She fixed her robe, gave him a kiss on the cheek, then went to bed with a smile on her face. Raphael went into the bathroom to wash up before getting into bed with Carla. She was still sound asleep when he got in bed.

He left the bedroom door open, and just as he was about to get up to close it, Elaina's frame appeared wearing nothing but her birthday suit. He opened his mouth to say something, but nothing came out. She lifted a leg up against the wall and stuck a finger into her pussy. Raphael kept trying to flag her off, but she kept going. His dick was getting hard all over again, and once she saw that it worked, she stopped and shut the door. He sighed then turned toward Carla, wrapping his arm around her and falling asleep.

TWELVE

"BOOK HIM ON AUTO theft, failing to obey a police officer's warning to stop, and possession of a controlled substance," the sergeant said to the desk officer.

Two other officers came out and grabbed the prisoner. They removed his handcuffs, and one officer frisked him, checking to make sure he didn't have anything on him. The other officer began taking inventory of his property. The prisoner noticed how busy everyone looked, and decided to use it to his advantage.

Theodore Gore was a four-time convicted felon, with two of them being gun convictions. He knew that if they ran his prints, he wasn't going anywhere anytime soon. He took that opportunity to make his move and reached for the officer's weapon. He punched the officer in the face and reached for the holster, yanking the gun from it.

"Go ahead, make my day," a plainclothes officer said, using her best Clint Eastwood impression. Her weapon aimed at the suspect's head.

He dropped the gun to the ground, then raised his hands in the air. Other police officers came from every direction and tackled him to the ground.

"Get him out of here, and you," she said, pointing to the officer whose lack of awareness almost resulted in tragedy, "get in my office now."

Without saying a word, the officer immediately walked with his head down to her office. She closed the door, chewed him out, then kicked him out of her office. She sat at her desk and started looking over some paperwork.

"I see you were the right pick for the job, Lieutenant Hill."

She looked up with a smile on her face, already knowing whose voice it was. Of course, it helped that they were partners for six years.

"What are you doing here?" she said, standing up to give him a hug.

"I just wanted to see if you were adapting to your new position, and from what I just seen, you're doing just fine," he said, releasing their embrace and sitting down.

"So what brings you here, Detective, or should I say Deputy Commissioner?" she asked, pouring herself a cup of coffee.

"It's not official yet, but we never had the chance to talk about that day, so I was thinking that maybe you would like to have dinner with me tonight. It's been a while, and like I told you when I was lying on that stretcher, no matter what, I have your back."

"You were my partner, Pete, but you requested a transfer with no explanation, and now I see why," she said with a smile.

"I had to make sure that you had some deception in your heart first before explaining my plans. Now that I know, we have some business to discuss. I'd rather not say anything here because it could be detrimental to both our careers. Meet me at my place, and I'll make dinner, okay?"

"You're cooking? I'll be there," she sarcastically said.

"Don't be smart, woman! I can still throw down in the kitchen. I have to go now, so see you later," he said, giving her a hug, then leaving the office.

She thought back to the day that she lost her lover when they tried to rob a basketball star's home. Her partner arrived on the scene and everything went crazy. A shootout erupted leaving two people dead and her partner in the hospital with a gunshot wound. He ended up alright, but it was what he said that stuck with her: "No matter what happens, I got your back."

Just as he had promised, he kept his word. Now that she had been promoted from a homicide detective to lieutenant, Cynthia knew she may have to do something to repay him but didn't know what. It didn't matter, though, because he had saved her job, and that was worth whatever he wanted.

"Lieutenant, we just received a call from the 1st Precinct. They are sending someone over to transport that prisoner," an officer said, peeping into her office.

He was wanted by a task force for multiple homicides in South Philly and had been on the run for six months.

"Get the paperwork ready for them," Lt. Hill replied.

"It's sitting at the front desk waiting for them. I'll make sure I drop it off to you as soon as they leave," the officer replied.

Lt. Hill finished her work and decided to head home. Since she and her husband separated, her days were mainly spent on the job. Since it was hot outside, she decided to take a swim in her pool, maybe even order some takeout and watch a good movie.

* * *

Around two o'clock in the morning, Kevin parked his car outside of a sports bar on Jerry's Corner, in Southwest Philly. He sat there patiently listening to the radio, waiting for his friend to arrive. A black SUV with tinted windows pulled up beside him and rolled down the window.

"Did I keep you waiting long?" the female driver asked, stepping out of the vehicle.

"No, I just pulled up!" he replied, unlocking the passenger door. "Get in!"

She got inside his car and pulled out a small package, passing it over to him. He opened it up to check the contents. After making sure it was what he wanted, he removed a large amount of cash from his pocket.

"This is stronger than the last stuff I gave you, so don't try to use it all at once," she told him as she counted the money that he just passed her.

"I'm a big boy. I assure you I can handle it!"

He rolled up a hundred-dollar bill, then placed more than the amount necessary onto a piece of cardboard that he pulled from the backseat. She watched him as he took a long hard sniff of the substance. Kevin's head shot straight back into the headrest, with his eyes looking like they were ready to pop out of his head. His breathing became irregular, and she could tell that the dosage was too much. When he started going into convulsions, she panicked and jumped out of the car. She took her cell phone out to make a call.

"Hello!" the caller said, answering after the first ring.

"It's done, but he took too much of the drug."

"What do you mean he took too much?"

"He's not moving!" she said, starting her vehicle.

"Get out of there. I have someone on their way to take care of it. This is only the beginning. We still have plenty of work ahead of us," the caller told her, ending the call.

As she pulled out of the lot, a utility van pulled up beside Kevin's car. Two men jumped out, grabbing Kevin and tossing his limp body inside. They left without any one of the pedestrians from the bar seeing them.

* * *

Mike saw Sasha outside collecting her mail from the mailbox, and walked in her direction. He didn't know what he was going to say, but he had to say something in defense of his father. She looked up just as he approached.

"I just wanted to apologize for my father's actions. He should have never broke the news to him like that. Is there anything I can do?"

"Yeah, just leave us alone and let me figure this out. He'll get what's coming to him," Sasha replied, looking through the letters.

"What's that supposed to mean?"

"Listen, Mike, I have a lot of things going on right now, and I don't have time to listen to you ranting on about what your father did. He said what he said, now me and my family will try to deal with it."

"It's our family too!" Mike stated. "Look, I didn't come over here to argue. I wanted to know if we could maybe get together tonight?"

"Mike, I told you before that we will not be doing that anymore. I'm trying to keep my family together," she told him.

"You weren't saying that at the restaurant!" he smirked, reaching for her hand.

Sasha quickly moved to the side, brushing him off. She gave him a look letting him know that she was serious about this affair ending.

"I said, that's enough!" she snapped.

"Fuck you, then! Have fun with your dysfunctional family, and I hope it works out for you," he said, walking away from her.

Sasha couldn't believe the way he was acting. It felt like déjà vu all over again from the last time she gave into his request, only this time they didn't have sex. Mike was seriously infatuated with Sasha, and even though he had been with plenty of other women, it was her that piqued his interest. Maybe it had something to do with the sex, or it was the fact that she was the older and more experienced woman that he couldn't have all to himself.

"Mike, don't you ever talk to me like that again."

"You know how I feel about you, Sasha, and you act like you don't feel the same way. Your husband just gonna continue to cheat on you when he's away, and you will be home wondering what it feels like to have a man in your bed at night," he stated, expecting her to lash out, but she didn't feed into his bullshit.

"It is none of your concern who sleeps in my bed at night. It won't be you, so get over it and move on with your life," she told him.

Sasha walked in the house and dropped the mail on the table. Her cell phone went off indicating that she had a message. It was a text from Marcus:

Hey baby,

I would like for you to meet me at our favorite restaurant tonight. I have something special planned for you to help take your mind off of things. Text me back if you're gonna be there.

♥*U*

Marcus

Sasha replied back to his message, informing him that she wouldn't be coming and that she needed to be home when Sahmeer woke up. Akiylah was out picking up groceries with her sister, so Sasha decided to take this time alone to get her mind right. She didn't know how badly the revealed secret would affect the relationship with her son, but she had to try to rekindle their bond. She poured herself a drink then sat on the couch until he came downstairs, so she could tell him everything. This burden was heavy on her mind and needed to be explained.

* * *

Akiylah was heading back to the mall to pick up her sister. Akiylah had received a phone call and had left her sister there for a few to meet up with a friend. Vanessa was standing outside smoking a Dutch when Akiylah pulled up. Akiylah was pissed at her sister for standing out there doing that in public.

"Me told you about smoking that shit in public. You not home, Nessa!" she said to her sister as soon as she closed the car door. "You can get arrested here for that, or get a hefty fine."

Vanessa smiled, feeling the effects of the loud. Her mind was in a whole new place, and she wasn't trying to let Akiylah ruin her mood. She sucked her teeth, then rolled her eyes as she looked through her bags, not paying Akiylah any attention.

"Do you want some?" Vanessa asked, passing Akiylah the Dutch.

Without saying a word, Akiylah took the Dutch and puffed on it three times. Vanessa laughed at her as she synced her phone to the car's Bluetooth. She hit a couple of buttons, and Buju Banton blazed through the speakers.

"That's me song, girl. Turn it up," Akiylah said, starting to feel the way her sister was feeling from the loud.

As they drove down I-76, traffic slowed down almost to a halt. This made Akiylah uncomfortable and impatient. She jumped on the right shoulder, weaving in and out of sitting traffic until she saw what was holding everyone up. She hit the brakes, but it was too late as she ran into the back of a disabled vehicle sitting on the side of the road.

"Oh my god, Akiylah, what have you done?" Vanessa said, panicking when she saw the passenger's head jerk forward.

Akiylah threw the car in park and hopped out, Vanessa following her. They walked over to check on the occupants. The lady that was sitting on the passenger side was holding her head in pain.

"Look over there!" Vanessa said, looking at the man with blood coming from his mouth lying on the ground in front of the vehicle. She walked over to where the man was squirming around, and kneeled down beside him. "Are you okay, sir?"

By this time, there were a couple of bystanders standing around watching with their camera phones out, recording the scene. Akiylah didn't know what do because this was her first time ever getting into an accident. She called Sahmeer, but he didn't answer his phone. Vanessa helped the man to their car and jumped in the driver's seat. Akiylah and the lady also got in, and they headed for the nearest emergency room.

By the time they reached University of Pennsylvania, there were about five police officers waiting for them. Akiylah was scared straight and knew that they were there for her. When they parked, two officers along with a medical team rushed over with a gurney and placed the injured man onto it.

"Miss, we need to get a statement from both of you real quick," a female officer said as she watched the man being rushed inside to surgery.

"She gave us a ride here! The person that hit him is still out there," the woman lied, trying to protect Akiylah and Vanessa.

They both looked at the lady in shock, wondering why she was taking up for them. Neither of them had the slightest idea of who she was; however, they were thankful for it.

"It's just procedure, ma'am. That's all. Can you describe what you seen and how the front of your vehicle was wrecked?" the officer asked pulling out her pad and pen to take notes.

The interrogation lasted about fifteen minutes; then Akiylah was allowed to leave. The lady came outside to speak with them after she talked to the doctor.

"They said he suffered lacerations in his right leg and a mild concussion, but he will be able to leave today."

"Me so sorry for hitting your car and friend. Is there any way me can repay you?" Vanessa stated, feeling guilty about it.

"Actually, there is something you can do for me, and we can call it even. You won't even have to worry about the cops getting involved in any kind of way," the lady said, staring at Vanessa.

"Just name it, and me will do it," she replied

"Well, can I speak with you in private for a minute?" the lady said, trying to hint to Vanessa to ditch her sister.

Vanessa picked up on her vibe and gave Akiylah a look saying that she'd be right back. Akiylah nodded her head because she wasn't trying to get arrested for fleeing the scene of an accident. Her biggest fear was what her husband would think, being that his family was in the spotlight. She didn't want to disappoint him, so whatever it took, she would do it.

"Me going to take a walk next door to get something to eat from McDonald's. Do you want me to bring you something?" Akiylah asked Vanessa.

"No, me good, Sis! We are going back inside to check on her husband and talk. If you need me, call me phone. We won't be long 'cause we have to get home," Vanessa stated, following the lady inside the hospital while Akiylah walked over to the children's hospital to get some food.

Vanessa followed the lady into the restroom hoping that it wouldn't take long. She could tell what the woman wanted by the way she kept staring at her. Truth be told, Vanessa wanted to taste her ever since she saw the way her ass looked in the skirt she had on. Even though Vanessa was only interested in men, she occasionally dabbled with the same sex.

"I saw the way you were looking at me, and you have me wet right now, see!" the lady said, lifting up her skirt, letting Vanessa see the wet spot coming from her twat.

Vanessa licked her lips, walking toward the lady, who was backing up into one of the stalls. The door shut behind them, and they were all over each other. Vanessa dipped a finger inside the woman's sopping wet pussy, then stuck it into her mouth. The lady let out a soft moan once she felt Vanessa stick it back inside.

"Get on your knees and eat my pussy," the lady said with authority, pushing Vanessa's head down.

She put her leg over Vanessa shoulder and closed her eyes as Vanessa devoured her insides. Vanessa licked and sucked on her clitoris, and stuck a finger in her asshole, driving the lady crazy.

"Oh my fucking god, I'm about to cum all over your face."

No sooner had she said it than her gushy load shot out like she had peed on herself. Vanessa sucked it all up and continued eating her out. When she came again, Vanessa began unbuttoning her pants.

"Wait, don't do that right now. I was just testing you out. Meet me at my house tonight and I'll explain everything," the lady said, passing Vanessa a card, then fixing her clothes and walking out with a smile on her face and feeling good.

* * *

When Kevin woke up, he tried to adjust his eyes to the darkness but couldn't see anything. The last thing he remembered was sniffing some raw and uncut dope, then everything going black. He didn't know it, but it was laced with something. Kevin had moved on from snorting coke, to snorting dope. Marcus told him that he needed to chill out from that stuff because it was affecting his game, but it wasn't that easy. Once the coke couldn't satisfy his urges anymore, that's when he switched. Now it was starting to become an addiction instead of a habit, and he knew it.

"So now you're on drugs, huh? Well let's see how you like what I have in store for you," someone said, startling him.

His eyes widened at the sound of the voice. Kevin thought he was hearing things, and started looking around trying to see who it was. When the lights came on and his eyes locked on the figure standing in front of him, he almost shit on himself.

"No, it can't be!" he said, looking into the person's eyes.

TO BE CONTINUED

"Text Good2Go at 31996 to receive new release updates via text message."

BOOKS BY GOOD2GO AUTHORS

GOOD 2 GO FILMS PRESENTS

THE HAND I WAS DEALT- FREE WEB SERIES

NOW AVAILABLE ON YOUTUBE!

YOUTUBE.COM/SILKWHITE212

SEASON TWO NOW AVAILABLE

To order books, please fill out the order form below:

To order films please go to www.good2gofilms.com

Name:_____

Address:_____

City: _____ State: _____ Zip Code: _____

Phone:_____

Email:_____

Method of Payment: Check   VISA   MASTERCARD

Credit Card#:_____

Name as it appears on card: _____

Signature: _____

Item Name	Price	Qty	Amount
48 Hours to Die – Silk White	$14.99		
A Hustler's Dream - Ernest Morris	$14.99		
A Hustler's Dream 2 - Ernest Morris	$14.99		
Bloody Mayhem Down South	$14.99		
Business Is Business – Silk White	$14.99		
Business Is Business 2 – Silk White	$14.99		
Business Is Business 3 – Silk White	$14.99		
Childhood Sweethearts – Jacob Spears	$14.99		
Childhood Sweethearts 2 – Jacob Spears	$14.99		
Childhood Sweethearts 3 - Jacob Spears	$14.99		
Childhood Sweethearts 4 - Jacob Spears	$14.99		
Flipping Numbers – Ernest Morris	$14.99		
Flipping Numbers 2 – Ernest Morris	$14.99		
He Loves Me, He Loves You Not - Mychea	$14.99		
He Loves Me, He Loves You Not 2 - Mychea	$14.99		
He Loves Me, He Loves You Not 3 - Mychea	$14.99		
He Loves Me, He Loves You Not 4 – Mychea	$14.99		
He Loves Me, He Loves You Not 5 – Mychea	$14.99		
Lord of My Land – Jay Morrison	$14.99		
Lost and Turned Out – Ernest Morris	$14.99		
Married To Da Streets – Silk White	$14.99		
M.E.R.C. - Make Every Rep Count Health and Fitness	$14.99		
My Besties – Asia Hill	$14.99		
My Besties 2 – Asia Hill	$14.99		
My Besties 3 – Asia Hill	$14.99		
My Besties 4 – Asia Hill	$14.99		
My Boyfriend's Wife - Mychea	$14.99		
My Boyfriend's Wife 2 – Mychea	$14.99		
Naughty Housewives – Ernest Morris	$14.99		
Naughty Housewives 2 – Ernest Morris	$14.99		

Naughty Housewives 3 – Ernest Morris	$14.99		
Never Be The Same – Silk White	$14.99		
Stranded – Silk White	$14.99		
Slumped – Jason Brent	$14.99		
Tears of a Hustler - Silk White	$14.99		
Tears of a Hustler 2 - Silk White	$14.99		
Tears of a Hustler 3 - Silk White	$14.99		
Tears of a Hustler 4- Silk White	$14.99		
Tears of a Hustler 5 – Silk White	$14.99		
Tears of a Hustler 6 – Silk White	$14.99		
The Panty Ripper - Reality Way	$14.99		
The Panty Ripper 3 – Reality Way	$14.99		
The Solution – Jay Morrison	$14.99		
The Teflon Queen – Silk White	$14.99		
The Teflon Queen 2 – Silk White	$14.99		
The Teflon Queen 3 – Silk White	$14.99		
The Teflon Queen 4 – Silk White	$14.99		
The Teflon Queen 5 – Silk White	$14.99		
The Teflon Queen 6 - Silk White	$14.99		
The Vacation – Silk White	$14.99		
Tied To A Boss - J.L. Rose	$14.99		
Tied To A Boss 2 - J.L. Rose	$14.99		
Tied To A Boss 3 - J.L. Rose	$14.99		
Tied To A Boss 4 - J.L. Rose	$14.99		
Time Is Money - Silk White	$14.99		
Two Mask One Heart – Jacob Spears and Trayvon Jackson	$14.99		
Two Mask One Heart 2 – Jacob Spears and Trayvon Jackson	$14.99		
Two Mask One Heart 3 – Jacob Spears and Trayvon Jackson	$14.99		
Young Goonz – Reality Way	$14.99		
Young Legend – J.L. Rose	$14.99		
Subtotal:			
Tax:			
Shipping (Free) U.S. Media Mail:			
Total:			

Make Checks Payable To:
Good2Go Publishing
7311 W Glass Lane,
Laveen, AZ 85339